AMELIA JANE AND THE SAILOR DOLL

and other stories

Illustrated by
Paul Crompton
and Joyce Johnson

World International Publishing Limited
Manchester

Copyright © 1991 Darrell Waters Limited.
This compilation 1991.
These stories were first published in Sunny Stories and Enid
Blyton's Magazine between 1928 and 1959.
Enid Blyton's signature is a Registered Trade Mark of
Darrell Waters Limited.

Published in Great Britain by World International
Publishing Limited,
An Egmont Company, Egmont House, PO Box 111,
Great Ducie Street,
Manchester M60 3BL.
Printed in Italy.

British Library Cataloguing in Publication Data
Blyton, Enid 1897–1968
Amelia Jane and the sailor doll and other stories.
I. Title
823.912 [J]

ISBN 0–7498–0297–9

Cover illustration by Robin Lawrie

Contents

Enid Blyton

Enid Blyton was born in London in 1897. Her childhood was spent in Beckenham, Kent, and as a child she began to write poems, stories and plays. She trained to be a teacher but she devoted her whole life to being a children's author. Her first book was a collection of poems for children, published in 1922. In 1926 she began to write a weekly magazine for children called *Sunny Stories*, and it was here that many of her most popular stories and characters first appeared. The magazine was immensely popular and in 1953 it became *The Enid Blyton Magazine*.

She wrote more than 600 books for children and many of her most popular series are still published all over the world. Her books have been translated into over 30 languages. Enid Blyton died in 1968.

Amelia Jane and the sailor doll

Once a new sailor doll came to the playroom where Amelia Jane and the rest of the toys lived. He was such a chatterbox.

"You know, sailors have adventures, plenty of them," he said. "And you should just hear mine . . ."

"We don't want to," said Amelia Jane. "You've told us about twenty times already."

"You're the rudest doll I've ever met," said the sailor doll huffily. "Well, as I was saying, one day when I was out at sea in my ship – I was the captain, of course – an enormous storm blew up, and the ship rocked to and fro, to and fro, just like a . . ."

"Rocking-horse," said Amelia with a giggle.

"Please be quiet," said the sailor. "Well, I somehow steered the ship to land and everyone was saved. Another time I went out in a lifeboat to rescue two people who couldn't swim. I got a medal for that. Look."

"It's not a medal," said Amelia Jane. "It's a button you picked up at the back of the toy cupboard. It's been there for ages."

"I don't believe you've ever *been* in a ship or a boat," said the clockwork mouse. "You just talk and talk."

Well, the sailor doll wasn't going to stand any rudeness from the mouse, and he chased him all round the room. Then he made a face at Amelia Jane and turned his back on her. He began talking all over again.

"*How* can we stop him from going on and on about adventures I'm sure he never had?" said the teddy bear. "He just goes on and on."

Well, Sailor went on like that till a day came when the children took the toys out into the garden for a picnic. They took little chairs and tables, too, for the toys to sit on, and gave them tiny cups of lemonade and plates full of biscuit crumbs. The toys really enjoyed themselves.

After the picnic, the children went indoors and left the toys by themselves. They were beside the little round pond where water-lilies floated on the water. Amelia Jane wanted to take off her shoes and paddle in the water. She called to the sailor doll.

"Come on, Sailor! You love the water, don't you? Let's paddle up to our knees, and you could take off your suit and have a swim, if you wanted to."

"I don't want to," said Sailor.

"You could sit on a water-lily leaf and have a very nice time," said Teddy.

"Don't be silly," said Sailor.

9

"Well, just come and wet your toes," said the pink rabbit. "Come on, you're always talking about what a wonderful life it is on the water. Here's plenty for you!"

"I'm sleepy," said the sailor doll. "Leave me alone. I wish there was somewhere soft and cosy to curl up – I'd have a nap in the sun."

Amelia Jane stared at him and a wicked look came into her eyes. "I know what you can do!" she said. "Look!"

She took hold of a toy table and turned it upside-down. She took some small cushions off the toy chairs and tucked them into the upside-down table. It looked a bit strange with its four legs sticking up into the air.

"A nice cosy bed for you!" said Amelia to Sailor. "Get in and have a nap. You *do* look tired."

Sailor was surprised to have so much kindness from Amelia Jane. He got into the table-bed and lay down. He yawned

loudly. "Nobody is to disturb me," he
said.

"No, Your Majesty," said the
clockwork mouse with a giggle.

Sailor frowned and closed his eyes.

"Don't disturb him," whispered
Amelia Jane to the others. "Let him go
fast asleep."

They were all puzzled. Why was Amelia being so nice to the sailor doll? Nobody liked him much. "I'll tell you in a minute," she whispered.

Soon the sailor doll began to snore. He often snored, and usually Amelia Jane tried to stop him. But she didn't this time. She tiptoed to the table-bed and smiled all over her face. She beckoned to Teddy, the clockwork mouse and the pink rabbit.

"We'll carry the upside-down table to the pond," she whispered. "And we'll set it floating on the water like a little boat. Whatever will he say when he wakes up?"

The clockwork mouse giggled so loudly that the bear gave him a sharp push. "Be quiet! You'll wake Sailor!"

Very gently the four toys each took one leg of the table and carried it to the pond. They set it down on the water, and Amelia gave it a push. It floated off beautifully to the middle of the pond, bumping into a yellow water-lily as it went. The goldfish were very surprised. They popped their red noses out of the water and had a good look.

"There he goes," said Amelia Jane with a chuckle. "He's got a boat at last! Hello, Captain! Hey, Captain, wake up, you're on a voyage to far away lands!"

The sailor doll woke up with a jump. He frowned. Hadn't he told the toys he wasn't to be disturbed? He turned over crossly on his cushions, and put one hand out over the edge of the floating table.

He got a sudden shock. Goodness! He had put his hand into something cold and wet! He sat up in a hurry.

He gazed round in fright. He was bobbing on the pond! Goodness gracious, what had happened! Why, the land seemed a long, long way away! He saw the toys standing on the edge of the pond, laughing.

"How did I get here?" he shouted. "Save me, quick!"

"You're the captain of your boat!" shouted Amelia. "You're sailing far away. You're having an adventure! Ooooh – mind a storm doesn't blow up!"

"I don't like it!" wailed Sailor, clinging to one of the table-legs. "I feel sick."

"He's sea-sick," said the clockwork mouse.

"No, pond-sick," said Teddy with a grin. "Our brave and wonderful Sailor, who has been through so many marvellous adventures, feels sea-sick on the pond. Hello – here comes the rain!"

Plop, plop, plop! Great raindrops fell on Sailor. The wind blew a little and ripples came on the pond. The table-boat bobbed up and down, and sailed all by itself into the very middle of the water-lilies.

"Help! Help!" yelled Sailor. "I shall drown! I shall fall in and drown!"

"Swim then!" shouted the rabbit, enjoying himself. "Swim like you say

14

you do when you go and rescue people."

"I can't swim!" wailed Sailor. "I can't, I can't! Save me!"

"The table's bobbing about on those little waves – I think it will turn over," said the clockwork mouse. "Sailor! Your boat may sink! Get out and sit on one of those water-lily leaves – they are so nice and flat!"

Sailor really was afraid that his table-boat would sink. He jumped on to a big, flat water-lily leaf. He sat down on it – and immediately it sank beneath him, and there he was, sitting in the water, yelling at the top of his voice.

"Goodness! He'll drown! He really and truly *can't* swim, for all the tales he's told us!" said the bear suddenly. "Look, he's slipping off that leaf – he's right in the water! I must save him!"

And, will you believe it, the fat old teddy bear suddenly plunged into the pond and began to swim as fast as he could towards poor old Sailor! Wasn't it brave of him?

Sailor clutched hold of him and Teddy swam back, puffing and panting. All the toys crowded round. They patted Teddy on his dripping wet back, and told him he was very, very brave.

"*I've* had an adventure now!" said Teddy, trying to squeeze water out of his furry little ears. "I swam out and saved somebody."

"Yes. But *your* adventure is a true one and Sailor's never are," said Amelia Jane. "Are they, Sailor?"

Sailor was standing all alone, his clothes making a puddle of wetness round his feet. He looked very much ashamed of himself. "Thank you, Teddy," he said in a small voice. "You were very brave – braver than I've ever been."

"That's the way to talk!" said the pink rabbit, pleased. "Come on – the sun's out again, so you and Teddy can sit in this sunny corner and get dry. Whatever will the children say if they find you dripping wet?"

Well, both Teddy and Sailor were dry when the children came back – but the little table still floated upside down on the pond! How surprised they were to see it there.

"Cushions in it, too!" they said. "What *have* the toys been up to?"

The toys didn't say a word, of course, but Amelia Jane looked even naughtier than usual.

And now, when Sailor forgets himself and begins one of his tales, Teddy interrupts at once, in a very loud voice, and begins his own tale.

"Once I swam out to rescue a silly sailor doll who couldn't even *swim*. It was a wonderful adventure for me. I'll tell you all about it."

And then, of course, Sailor stops boasting at once and creeps away. A sailor doll who couldn't swim! He will never, never be allowed to forget that.

What naughty things you do, Amelia Jane! However do you think of them?

Amelia Jane again!

D o you remember Amelia Jane, the doll who didn't know how to behave herself because she was homemade, and didn't come from a shop?

Well, for a long time she was very good – and then, oh dear, she forgot all her promises and became really naughty! The things she did!

She took a needle and cotton out of the workbasket and sewed up the sleeves of the teddy bear's new coat when he wasn't looking. So when he went to put on his coat, he simply could *not* put his arms through the sleeves at all! They just couldn't find the way in – because the sleeves were sewn up! How Amelia Jane laughed to see him!

The next night she hid behind the curtain and began to mew like a cat. The toys were not very fond of Tibs the cat, because he sometimes chewed them. So they all stopped playing and looked round to see where Tibs was.

"I can hear him mewing!" said the teddy bear. "He must be behind the door."

But he wasn't. Amelia mewed again. The toys hunted all about for the cat. They even looked under the rug, which made Amelia laugh till she nearly choked! She mewed again, very loudly.

"Where *is* that cat?" cried the pink rabbit in despair. "We've looked everywhere! Is he behind the curtain?"

"No, there's only Amelia Jane there!" said the curly-haired doll, looking. "There's no cat."

Well, of course, they didn't find any cat at all! And Amelia Jane didn't tell them it was she who had been mewing, so to this day they wonder where Tibs hid herself that night!

Then Amelia Jane saw a soda water syphon left in a corner of the room. She knew how they worked, because she had seen someone using one. Oh, what fun it would be to squirt all the toys! She stole towards it and picked it up. Dear me, it *was* heavy! She ran at the surprised pink rabbit, pressed down the handle – and out gushed the soda water all over him!

"Ow! Ooh!" he shouted, in astonishment. "What is it! What is it! Amelia Jane, you ought to be ashamed of yourself!"

But she wasn't a bit ashamed. She was enjoying herself thoroughly! She ran after the teddy bear and soaked him with soda water too. She squirted lots over the clockwork mouse, and made him so wet that for two days his clockwork went wrong, and he couldn't be wound up. She squirted the pink rabbit again and he got into the waste-paper basket and couldn't get out, which worried him very much because he was so afraid that he would be thrown away the next day! Luckily, he wasn't.

"Amelia Jane is up to her tricks again," said the clockwork clown, frowning. "We shall have no peace at all. What shall we do?"

"Take away her key!" said the clockwork mouse.

"She hasn't one, silly!" said the curly-haired doll.

"Lock her in the cupboard!" said the teddy bear.

"She knows how to undo it from the inside," said the pink rabbit gloomily.

Nobody spoke for a whole minute. They were all thinking hard.

Then the clockwork clown gave a little laugh. "I know!" he said. "I've thought of an idea. It's quite simple, but it might work."

"What?" cried everyone.

"Let's polish Amelia Jane's shoes underneath and make them very, very slippery," said the clown. "Then, if she begins to run after us with soda water syphons or things like that, down she'll go!"

"But she won't like that," said the curly-haired doll, who was rather tender-hearted.

"Well, *we* don't like the tricks she plays on *us*!" said the teddy bear. "We'll do it, Clown! When she next takes her shoes off we'll polish them underneath till they are as slippery as glass!"

The very next night Amelia Jane took off her shoes because her feet were hot. She put the shoes into a corner and then danced round the playroom in her socks, enjoying herself. The clown picked up the shoes and ran away to the back of the toy cupboard with them. He had a tiny duster there, and a little bit of polish he had taken out of the polish jar when the playroom had been cleaned out.

Aha, Amelia Jane, you'll be sorry for all your tricks! The clown polished and rubbed, rubbed and polished. The soles of the shoes shone. They were as slippery as could be! The clown put them back and waited for Amelia Jane to put them on. This she very soon did, for she stepped on a pin and pricked her foot! She ran to put on her shoes. As she put them on, she thought out a naughty trick!

"I'll run after all the toys with that pin I trod on!" she thought. "Oooh! That will make them rush away into all the corners! What fun it will be to frighten them!"

She buttoned her shoes and took the nasty long pin. Then she stood up and looked round, her naughty black eyes gleaming. "I'll run after that fat little teddy bear!" she thought. So off she went, straight at the teddy bear, holding the pin out in front of her.

"Amelia Jane, put that pin down!" shouted the teddy bear in fright – but before Amelia Jane had taken three steps, her very, very slippery shoes slid along the ground and down she fell, bumpity-bump! She *was* surprised!

Up she got again and took a few more steps towards the teddy bear – but her shoes slipped and down she fell! Bumpity-bump!

"What's the matter with the carpet?" cried Amelia Jane, in a rage. "It keeps making me fall down!"

"Ha ha! ho ho!" laughed the toys. "Perhaps there is slippery magic about, Amelia Jane!"

"Oh, I believe you toys have something to do with it!" shouted the angry doll. Up she got and took the pin in her hand again. "I'll show you what happens to people who put slippery magic on the floor! Here comes my pin!"

She tried to run at the pink rabbit, who was laughing so much that pink tears ran all down his face. But down she went again, bumpity-bump – and oh my, the pin stuck into her knee! Yes, it really did – she fell on it!

How Amelia Jane squealed! How Amelia Jane wept! "Oh, the horrid pin! Oh, how it hurts!" she cried.

"Well, Amelia Jane, it serves you right," said the pink rabbit. "You were going to prick *us* with that pin and now it's pricked *you*! You know how it feels!"

Amelia Jane threw the pin away in a rage. The clown picked it up and threw it into the waste-paper basket. He wasn't going to have pins about the playroom!

Amelia Jane got up again. "I'm going to bandage my knee where the pin pricked it," she said. She ran to the toy cupboard – but before she was half-way there, her slippery shoes slid away beneath her – and down she sat with a dreadful bumpity-bumpity-bump!

The toys laughed. Amelia Jane cried bitterly. The curly-haired doll felt sorry for her. "Don't cry any more, Amelia Jane," she said. "Take your shoes off and you won't fall any more. We played a trick on you – but you can't complain because you have so often tricked *us*! You should not play jokes on other people if you can't take a joke yourself!"

Amelia Jane took her shoes off. She saw how the clown had polished them underneath, and she went very red. She knew quite well she could not grumble if people were unkind – because she too had been unkind.

"I'll try and be good, toys," she said, at last. "It's difficult for me, because I'm not a shop toy like you, so I haven't learnt good manners and nice ways. But I may be good one day!"

The toys thought it was nice of her to say all that. The curly-haired doll came to help her bandage her knee. She looked so funny that they didn't know whether to laugh or cry at her.

Amelia Jane did enjoy being fussed! She is as nice as can be to the toys now – but oh dear, oh dear, I do somehow feel perfectly certain it won't last long! I'll tell you if it doesn't.

Amelia Jane in trouble again

Once upon a time Amelia Jane, the big, naughty doll, was taken down to the seaside with some of the other toys. The clockwork clown went, the brown teddy bear, the pink rabbit and the golden-haired doll. They went in the car with the children, and they were all most excited.

"I shall dig in the sand and throw it over everybody!" said naughty Amelia Jane. "And I shall get my pail and fill it full of water and pour it down the rabbit's neck! Ho, won't he jump!"

"You'll do nothing of the sort, Amelia Jane," said the pink rabbit at once. "You know how often you've promised to be good. Well, just you remember your promise."

"And I shall push the clockwork clown into a rockpool and make him sit down there with all his clothes on," said Amelia Jane, with a naughty giggle.

"You mustn't!" cried the clown, in alarm. "If you do that my clockwork will get rusty and I shan't wind up properly – then I won't be able to walk any more, or turn head-over-heels!"

The children often took the toys down to the beach with them. After dinner, the children went to have a rest, and the toys were left in a sheltered corner of the beach. No one ever came there, so the children knew they were quite safe. And it was whilst the toys were left alone there that Amelia Jane behaved so very badly. She did all she said she would, and more too.

She threw sand all over the golden-haired doll, and it went into her eyes dreadfully. She cried, and the pink rabbit had to find his handkerchief and comfort her. Whilst he was patting the doll on the back, and wiping the sand out of her eyes, Amelia Jane was filling her pail from a pool.

She crept up behind the pink rabbit – and tipped the pail of cold sea water all down his neck!

"Ooooo-ow-oooo!" yelled the pink rabbit jumping about twelve inches into the air with fright. "You wicked doll, Amelia Jane! I told you not to do that!"

Amelia Jane thought it was such a funny joke that she rolled over and over on the sand with laughing. The clockwork clown, who had seen all that had happened, remembered what she had said she would do to him, and he ran away to hide. He really was dreadfully afraid Amelia Jane would push him into a pool. Amelia looked for him. He had hidden himself under a clump of seaweed, so she couldn't see him – but she saw the brown teddy bear!

He was walking round the edge of a fine deep pool, looking at the crabs there. Amelia Jane crept up behind him. She gave him a push – SPLASH! The teddy landed in the pool and sat right down in the water.

"Oooooo-ow-ooooo!" he gasped, his mouth full of salty water. Amelia Jane laughed till the tears ran down her face.

"You are very naughty and unkind," said the clockwork clown, poking his head out of the seaweed nearby. "You are a most dreadful doll. Hi, rabbit, come and help me push Amelia Jane into the water!"

"I shan't let you!" said Amelia Jane, at once. "I shall paddle out to sea and sit on that rock over there. I am bigger than any of you, and I can get through the deep water easily. You won't be able to follow me. I shall be quite safe. Ha,ha, to you, clockwork clown!"

Amelia Jane had no shoes or socks on. She lifted up her red skirt and stepped into the waves. She waded out towards the big, big rock that showed itself some way out. It was covered with green seaweed. The teddy shook the water from his fur and ran after Amelia, splashing through the waves. But he was afraid of getting drowned, and he soon came back. Amelia was a very big doll, so she could easily get to the rock. The water did not come to more than her knees.

She reached the rock and climbed up. She waved to the others.

"I'm the king of the castle!" she shouted, dancing on the rock. "You can't get me! I shall stay here and have a nice nap!"

She lay down on the green, soft seaweed. The hot sun had dried it well. It was like a soft bed.

Amelia fell asleep. When the children came out to play, they didn't miss her. They had new spades and they wanted to dig a big castle. They took no notice of any of the other toys, and didn't even see how wet the teddy bear was. They dug and dug and dug.

They had tea on the beach and then they dug again. When it was time to go home, they collected their toys and set off up the beach. They had the clockwork clown, the bear, the pink rabbit and the golden-haired doll – but they didn't have Amelia Jane. They had forgotten all about her.

And what about Amelia Jane? She was still asleep on the rock! The tide was now coming in – and it crept higher and higher over the rock. Soon it would reach Amelia's toes. Soon a big wave would break right over the rock on top of Amelia – and then what would happen to her?

Amelia woke up. She sat up on the rock and looked round. When she saw how the tide was coming in, she was in a dreadful fright. The water was too deep to paddle through now. She couldn't swim. Oh dear!

Amelia Jane stood and yelled for help.

"Save me, somebody," she cried. "Save me!" But there was no one to save her. Poor Amelia Jane!

The other toys were sitting on a shelf, watching the children go to bed. Nobody thought of Amelia Jane. They were only too glad to forget her.

But when the children were safely in bed, the pink rabbit suddenly looked round – and saw no Amelia. For a moment he wondered where she was – and then he remembered! She had been left on the rock – and the tide was coming in. Oooooo!

"Oh, toys," said the rabbit, "Amelia Jane's on the rock – and the tide will soon cover it!"

Now you might think that the clown, the golden-haired doll and the rabbit would say, "And serve Amelia right!" – but they didn't. They all looked at one another in alarm. Amelia was naughty – and she had played tricks on them – but they could not let anything horrid happen to her.

"What can we do?" asked the clown. He got down from the shelf and ran to the window. From there he could quite well see the rock on which Amelia stood, shouting for help.

"We must save her!" said the golden-haired doll.

"But how?" asked the pink rabbit.

"I know!" said the clown suddenly. "We will take the children's toy ship —

36

and sail it to the rock. We shall just get there in time. Hurry!"

The rabbit and the clown caught hold of the toy ship, which lay on the floor. They ran out of the door with the golden-haired doll, and tore down to the beach. They put the boat into the water.

The rabbit got in. The golden-haired doll got in. The clockwork clown pushed off, and then jumped in himself. The rabbit arranged the white sails so that the wind filled them. The clown took the rudder and guided the little ship.

The tide was coming in fast. It was a long, long way now to the rock. Amelia Jane was very frightened. A big wave had washed right over the rock and had wet her to the waist. Amelia was afraid that the next one would wash her right off the rock into the big sea.

"Help! Help!" she shouted, as another big wave came over the rock. Amelia held on to some seaweed. The sea wet her right up to her shoulders. Oooh! It was so cold! She knew now how cold the pink rabbit must have felt when she poured water down his neck that morning!

"We're coming, Amelia Jane; we're coming!" shouted the toys. Amelia Jane heard them. She looked over the waves and saw the three toys in the sailing-ship. It bobbed up and down as it came, for the sea was quite rough.

"Oh, you good toys!" sobbed Amelia Jane. "I don't deserve to be rescued – I was so unkind to you – but oh, I'm *so* glad to see you!"

The ship sailed quite near to the rock. The clown was careful not to let it strike the rock – for that would mean a wreck. "Jump, Amelia, jump into the ship!" he called. "We can't come any nearer!"

Amelia Jane jumped. It was a good jump. She landed right in the middle of the boat. It swayed about, and then as the clown turned it into the wind, the sails filled and the little ship sailed towards the shore again.

"You'll soon be safe at home," said the golden-haired doll kindly. "Don't cry, Amelia Jane."

"I won't tease you any more, any of you," wept Amelia. "It was so kind of you to remember I was on the rock and come to rescue me. Thank you ever and ever so much."

The ship reached the sand. The rabbit jumped out and pulled it in. The golden-haired doll jumped out and helped poor, wet, cold Amelia Jane out. The clown jumped out last of all – and then they carried the ship back to the playroom again.

The rabbit took Amelia Jane to the bathroom and dried her. Then back to the playroom they went, and soon fell asleep after their exciting day.

And was Amelia Jane kinder to the toys after that? Yes, very much kinder, all the time they were away at the seaside. They are back home again now – and Amelia Jane will soon forget her good ways, I expect. Don't you?

The little girl who cried

"Anna's always got red eyes," said Lucy. "She's a baby. She's always crying."

"Cry-baby, cry-baby!" said Katie, pointing her finger at Anna, who was coming along wiping her eyes. She had just fallen down and hurt her knee.

That made Anna begin to cry all over again. She really was a cry-baby, but she hated being called one.

Poor Anna! She cried if she fell down. She cried if her porridge was too hot. She cried if she made a mistake in her writing book. She cried if she thought she was going to be late for school, and she cried if anyone scolded her.

"For goodness sake, Anna, don't turn

on the tap again!" said Lucy. "Where do you get all your tears from? I never knew anyone cry such buckets of tears. You should do very, very well as a watering-can."

Everybody laughed except Anna. She wept a few more tears. "You're unkind," she said. "You *make* me cry. I'm very unhappy."

"You're a little silly," said Katie. "You just *let* yourself cry! *We* could cry, too, when we fall down and hurt ourselves – but we don't. We just press our lips together hard and get up and rub our knees and go on playing. We won't *let* ourselves cry."

The children teased poor Anna a good deal. It really was quite a joke with them to make Anna cry. It was so easy!

"If anyone jumps out and says 'BOO!' Anna cries," said Lucy. "And if you say 'Silly-Billy' she cries. And if you take away her pencil she cries. Let's tease her and get her out of the habit of crying. It's the only way."

But it wasn't a good way with Anna. She grew frightened of the others, and began to hate going to school. She seemed to cry all day long and her teacher was worried about her.

So one day she asked Anna to tea, and Anna went. There were crumpets for tea, well toasted, and a homemade chocolate cake, and homemade strawberry jam. So Anna enjoyed herself and for a whole hour not a single tear came into her eyes.

After tea Miss Brown pulled two chairs up to the fire and began to talk.

"You know, Anna," she said, "I really am pleased that you haven't cried yet. You look so nice when you are smiling, and your eyes are bright and merry, instead of being full of tears and sad."

Anna looked at herself in the mirror. Yes, she certainly did look nicer. But even as she thought of how the others teased her and made her cry, the tears came into her eyes!

"Well, if you haven't begun again!" said Miss Brown, laughing. "What shall we do with you? I believe you *like* crying, Anna."

"Oh, I don't, I don't," said Anna at once. "I'm ashamed of it, I really am. I hate being a cry-baby. But I suppose I always shall be."

"You certainly will if you think like that," said Miss Brown. "We make ourselves what we are, you know."

"But I don't know how to stop," said poor Anna. "Oh, how I wish I was someone brave and great and fearless, not myself."

"I know what you could do!" said Miss Brown. "You could pretend to be Anna the Fearless!"

"Who was she?" said Anna in surprise. "I've never heard of her."

"She was a very brave peasant-girl in a far-off country," said Miss Brown. "Enemies came to look for her father and brothers, who were hiding in a wood nearby. They found Anna and tried to make her say where they were."

"And did she?" said Anna.

"No," said Miss Brown. "So the enemy thought they would treat her cruelly, make her cry bitterly, and then perhaps she would give her people away. So they beat her, but Anna didn't cry a single tear."

"She was brave," said Anna.

"She was proud," said Miss Brown, "too proud to weep. She did not mean to show her enemies that they hurt her. So she stood there, her mouth tight shut, her face white, but she did not let a single tear trickle down her cheek in case the enemy thought she was weakening. Then they burnt down her house, but even when she saw the flames Anna would not give away her father and brothers, nor beg for mercy, nor cry."

"Oh, Miss Brown – she *must* have been brave!" said Anna, her eyes shining. "What happened then?"

"The enemy said they were sure the little girl did not know where her father and brothers were, or she would certainly have told them, or cried bitterly," said Miss Brown. "So they left her there and went away. And her father and brothers came out of their hiding-place, and hugged her and praised her for her fearlessness and loyalty."

"I wish I was that Anna," said Anna. "Oh, how I wish I was as brave as that."

"Do you really?" said Miss Brown. "Well, listen, Anna. You can never be *that* little Anna because you are yourself and always will be. But why don't you *pretend* to be that other Anna, when people tease you, or you fall down and hurt yourself, or things go wrong? Say to yourself then, 'I am Anna the Fearless and I will not cry!' I don't believe you will be able to weep a single tear if you do that."

"Oh, Miss Brown, I'll try it!" said Anna in delight. "I really will. If I *pretend* to be brave, that's the next best thing to *being* brave, isn't it?"

"It's very often the same thing!" said Miss Brown. "Now go home and think about it. I hope by the end of the term that I really shall have a little Anna the Fearless in my class."

Anna felt excited. She went home. She thought about it. She went to bed and dreamed about it. She *would* be like Anna the Fearless, she would!

She set off to school, and met Lucy and Katie. "Hallo, here's the silly cry-baby!" said Lucy. "Pull her hair!"

They pulled Anna's hair, but she

46

pursed up her lips and pulled her head away from them. "I'm Anna the Fearless!" she thought to herself. "What do I care for enemies? What do I care about bad names and pulled hair? Nothing at all. I'm Anna the Fearless."

So, to the great surprise of the others, not a tear rolled down Anna's cheek. They all went on to school talking. Just as they got to the school-gate Harry came along and pushed Anna roughly

against the gate-post. She grazed her arm, and tears sprang to her eyes. But at once she spoke to herself proudly.

"I'm Anna the Fearless! What do I care about a silly grazed arm? Nothing at all. My enemies shall never make me cry!"

So she blinked back the tears and not one rolled down her cheek. Harry was surprised.

"No tears this morning?" he said. "What's happened to our cry-baby?"

The bell rang and the children ran to take their places. School began, and lesson after lesson was taken.

In writing-lesson John jogged Anna's arm, and her pen shot across the page and spoilt her work. Usually Anna would have wailed aloud, cried bitterly, and told tales. But today she glared at John, pursed up her lips, and said nothing. John waited to see the tears come, but none came. Anna the Fearless was not going to cry over a little thing like that.

At playtime the children rushed out, laughing and shouting. They played catch in the garden, and had a fine time. The day was rather wet, and the ground was muddy. As she ran, Anna slipped and fell. She hurt both her knees and one hand. She got up at once, and the others crowded round her, expecting to see floods of tears, and to hear loud yells.

"Bother," said Anna in a loud, clear voice. "Now my knees are bleeding, and I'll have to wash them."

"One's quite bad, Anna," said Lucy, feeling sorry. "Poor old Anna. Never mind."

The kind words almost made Anna cry. But she held up her head proudly. "I'm Anna the Fearless," she thought. "I don't cry about hurt knees and hands. Nobody can make me cry if I don't want to. My enemies shall never see me cry. I'm brave and fearless, and I've more courage than all the others put together."

Her knees hurt her and her hand bled. But she even managed a funny little smile when Miss Brown bathed the bruises and bandaged her knees.

"You're Anna the Fearless, aren't you?" whispered Miss Brown. "I thought you were. Anna, you are marvellous. Keep it up, won't you?"

"It's fun to pretend I am what I'm not when it's something so much grander and better than myself," said Anna. "I know I'm a baby, and silly and weak, but I feel fine when I'm pretending to be brave and grand."

Miss Brown smiled a secret little smile. "You will find it isn't all pretence, if you keep it up long enough," she said.

"I'll keep it up till the end of the term, then I think I'll have a rest, and be myself in the holidays," said Anna. "It's really not very easy, you know, Miss Brown, although it's fun. I'll go back to being silly again in the holidays, but in school I'll always be Anna the Fearless now."

So she went on being Anna the Fearless for the rest of the term, and soon the children gave up teasing her, because it wasn't any fun. Anna didn't cry any more. She was braver than the biggest child. She didn't seem to care when she was hurt or teased. The children thought she was quite different and very much nicer.

"And now, Anna, I suppose you won't be Anna the Fearless after today," said Miss Brown at the end of the term. "You'll be the poor little frightened Anna I knew at the beginning of the term."

"I expect so," said Anna. "I've tried very hard, Miss Brown, and now I want a rest. I shan't be Anna the Fearless in the holidays."

But wasn't it an extraordinary thing? Anna couldn't stop being Anna the Fearless! She had pretended to be brave and courageous so long that now she really was. She couldn't cry at little things. It was natural for her to be brave now. She could never, never be cry-baby Anna again.

"Well, what a funny thing," said Anna, and she ran to tell Miss Brown after three days of the holidays. Miss Brown smiled.

"I rather thought this would happen," she said, giving Anna a hug. "I told you we make our own selves what we are, didn't I? Brave or cowardly, kind or selfish, good or bad. Well, you made yourself different by acting like somebody else. You really are a little Anna the Fearless now, and always will be. I'm proud of you, Anna; really proud of you. You need never be afraid of being a cry-baby again."

I know Anna very well, and she is one of the finest, bravest children I know; but she certainly wasn't always like that. It's a very good idea of Miss Brown's, isn't it – to pretend to be someone braver, or kinder or stronger than yourself? Because, you always end up really being like that!

Pippitty's pet canary

Little Princess Pippitty had a beautiful yellow canary called Goldie. She loved it very much, and looked after it every day. She loved it far better than any of her other pets, and when the King and Queen took her away to the seaside for a holiday she wanted to take Goldie too.

"No, you can't do that," said the Queen. "Goldie must stay behind with all your dogs and cats and ponies. We will ask Gobbo the elf to look after Goldie for you."

"But suppose he lets Goldie fly away!" cried Pippitty. "It would break my heart, really it would."

"Well, if he lets your canary escape, he will be punished!" said the King. "Now cheer up, Pippitty – you may be sure Gobbo will look after Goldie very well indeed."

The day came for the King and Queen and Pippitty to start off in the golden coach. Pippitty said goodbye to all her pets, and kissed her canary on his little yellow beak.

"See that you look after Goldie well, Gobbo," said the King. "Feed him every day, give him fresh water to drink and to bathe in, and clean out his cage – and whatever you do, don't let him fly away! If you let him escape, you will be punished!"

"I will look after him well," promised Gobbo, and he bowed very low. Then the Princess blew a last kiss to her canary, and stepped into the golden coach. Off they all went to the seaside.

Gobbo went to the canary's cage every day, and did all that he had been told to do. Goldie missed the Princess, and sat all day long on his perch, moping. Gobbo tried to cheer him up, but it was no use.

"Where's the Princess?" Goldie kept asking. "Where's Pippitty? Let me out, Gobbo, and I will go and look for her."

"Oh no, I mustn't let you out," said Gobbo. "Be patient, Goldie. Pippitty will be back soon. I should be punished if I let you out of your cage."

The time went by, and at last came the day when Princess Pippitty was to come back home again. Gobbo went to Goldie's cage and cleaned it out beautifully. Then he polished the bars till they shone like gold.

"You haven't given me enough water to bathe in," complained Goldie. "I shall tell Pippitty when she comes back."

"Pippitty is coming back today," said Gobbo.

"Oh, I don't believe you!" said the canary. "You keep saying she will be back soon, she will be back soon, and she doesn't come. Give me some more water to bathe in."

Gobbo opened the door of the cage, and he was just going to put some more water in, when someone at the door called: "Gobbo! Gobbo! Come quickly and see the rainbow!"

Gobbo put the water down quickly and ran to the window – and oh dear, he forgot to shut the cage door! In a trice Goldie was out of the cage and flying round the room. Gobbo shut the window with a bang, and then ran to shut the door. The canary could not get out of the room.

Gobbo's friend, Peepo, the one who had told him to look at the rainbow, stared at Gobbo in surprise.

"What are you shutting the doors and windows for?" he asked. "Do you feel cold?"

"No," said Gobbo, "but don't you see that Goldie the canary has escaped? I shall be punished if the Princess comes back and sees him out of his cage."

"Oh my, oh my!" said Peepo in dismay. "Do go back to your cage, Goldie."

"Oh no!" said Goldie. "Once out of my cage I'll never go back! I'll just wait till the Princess comes and then I'll fly down to her shoulder and ask her to let me be free."

"You would die if you flew out of doors like the other birds," said Gobbo. "You don't know how to find your own food. Be a sensible little bird and go back to your beautiful big cage."

But Goldie wouldn't. Gobbo began to cry, for he felt quite certain that the King and Queen would be cross. Peepo sighed in despair, for he knew that if only he hadn't called Gobbo to look at the rainbow, his friend wouldn't have let the canary escape.

Suddenly there came a knock at the door and in came Merry-one the jester. The canary flew to the door to get out, but Merry-one shut it just in time.

"Hallo, hallo!" he said in surprise. "What's this I see? Goldie out of his cage! I fear you will be punished for this, Gobbo."

"Oh, Merry-one, help me to get Goldie back!" begged Gobbo, the tears running down his cheeks.

"How did he get out?" asked Merry-one.

"Well, you see," said Gobbo, "I was just giving Goldie some more water, when Peepo called out to me to go and see the rainbow, and while I was looking, Goldie —"

"Wait a minute, wait a minute!" said Merry-one, looking puzzled. "I'm getting muddled. Now, let's begin again. Goldie was giving Peepo some water, and you saw a rainbow?"

"No, no," said Gobbo. "*I* was giving Goldie some water, and Peepo called out —"

"Where was Peepo?" asked Merry-one, looking more puzzled than ever. "Was he in the cage?"

"No, *I* was in the cage, you stupid creature!" cried the canary.

"Oh, *you* were in the cage," said Merry-one. "Well, Peepo was giving you some water, and Gobbo called out to him to see a rainbow, and —"

"No, no, *no!*" said Gobbo and Peepo together. "You've got it all wrong."

"You *are* stupid!" said the canary, fluttering its wings crossly. "Begin at the beginning, now. I was in the cage."

"Yes," said Merry-one. "I was in the cage — no, no, that's wrong, of course. Gobbo was in the cage, and Goldie

59

was – no, that's wrong too. Oh my, I'm getting so muddled I shall never, never understand this!"

"I'll *make* you understand!" cried the canary in a rage. "Look here, *I* was in the cage – like this –" and Goldie flew back into his cage, and stood on the perch. "Do you understand that, Merry-one?"

"Perfectly, thank you!" cried the jester, and he banged the cage door shut. "*You* were in the cage, Goldie, ha, ha! And you are in the cage now! Ho, ho! Oh yes, I understand all right and so do the others, I'm sure!"

"Ha, ha!" roared Gobbo and Peepo, joyfully. "Oh, Merry-one, we thought you were being so stupid, and really you were as clever as could be!"

"Oh thank you, thank you for saving my head for me!" said Gobbo, and he shook Merry-one gratefully by the hand.

Goldie the canary flew into a terrible rage and shook the bars of his cage till they rattled – but nobody took any notice. They had heard the sound of cheering outside.

"The Princess! The King and Queen!" cried Peepo and Gobbo, and they rushed to the window. Sure enough, there was the golden coach, and as the three watched, the King and the Queen stepped out, and little Princess Pippitty followed.

And the very first thing she did was to rush upstairs to see Goldie her canary! Wasn't it a good thing he was safely back in his cage? He was so delighted to see Pippitty that he forgot all about his bad temper, and sang her a beautiful song of welcome.

Nobody told tales on Gobbo, so he was quite safe – but dear me, didn't he have a narrow escape?

Mary Brown and Mary Contrary

Mary was out for a walk. She took with her Josephine, her biggest doll, and wheeled her in her pram. It was a lovely day, and the sun shone brightly.

Mary went a long way. She walked down the little green path in Bluebell Wood to get out of the hot sun — but dear me, when she turned back, she found that she had lost her way!

Somehow or other she must have taken the wrong path — and now she didn't know how to get back. She was most upset.

"Never mind," she said to herself. "I

shall soon meet someone, and then I can ask them the way to my home."

In a few minutes she *did* meet someone. It was a little fat man in a green tunic. He was hurrying along with a white hen under his arm. Mary called to him.

"Please," she said, "I've lost my way. Can you tell me how to get home?"

"What is your name?" asked the fat man.

"I'm Mary," said the little girl. "And this is Josephine, one of my dolls."

"How do you do, Mary, how do you do, Josephine?" said the little man, raising his pointed cap, politely. "Yes, certainly I can show you your way home. Come with me."

Mary followed him through the wood, pushing Josephine before her in her pram. She walked down the narrow green path – and at last, to her great surprise, she came out into a little village.

What a strange village! The cottages

were very tiny indeed, and at the doors
and in the gardens stood children
dressed in strange suits and dresses.
They looked just as if they had come
out of her nursery rhyme book.

"Those two might be Jack and Jill!"
thought Mary, looking at a boy and girl
who stood holding a pail between them.
"And that boy singing all by himself

there is just like Tommy Tucker. Look at that tiny girl sitting on a stool too – she's just like Miss Muffet eating her curds and whey!"

"We're nearly there," said the little man.

"I don't seem to know this way home," Mary said.

"Don't you?" asked the fat man in surprise, and his hen clucked loudly under his arm, as if she too was surprised. "Well – here you are. There's your cottage, look!"

Mary looked. They had stopped just outside a trim little cottage, whose walls were painted white. At the windows hung pretty curtains, and the door was painted bright yellow. It was a dear little cottage.

"But that isn't my home!" said Mary. "You've made a mistake!"

"Well, didn't you say that you were Mary?" asked the little man, in astonishment. "This is Mary's cottage. Look, there's the name on the gate."

Mary looked. Sure enough on the gate the words 'MARY'S COTTAGE' were painted.

"And look – there are your cockle shells making a nice border to your flower-beds," said the little man, pointing. "And there are your pretty Canterbury Bells, all flowering nicely in the sunshine."

Mary stared at the cottage garden. She saw that each flower-bed was neatly edged with cockle-shells, and that wonderful Canterbury Bells flowered everywhere, their blossoms just like silver bells, instead of being blue or white.

"And there are your pretty maids all in a row!" said the little man, waving his hand to where a row of pretty dolls sat on the grass. "Look, your doll wants to join them."

To Mary's great astonishment she saw her doll Josephine getting out of the pram! Josephine walked through the garden gate and sat herself down in the row of dolls, who seemed very pleased to see her. Then the wind blew and all the Canterbury Bells began to ring – tinkle – tinkle – tinkle!

Mary was too surprised to speak. She couldn't understand it at all – and yet she felt she had seen all this before somewhere – was it in a book?

"*Isn't* this your home?" asked the little man, looking puzzled. "Your name is Mary, Mary, Quite Contrary, isn't it?"

"No, it isn't!" cried Mary, seeing where he had made his mistake. "I'm just Mary Brown! You thought I was some other Mary – the Mary of the nursery rhyme. *You* know, Mary, Mary, Quite Contrary, How does your garden grow? With silver bells and cockle-shells, And pretty maids all in a row!"

"Well, of *course* I thought you were!" said the little man. "I'm so sorry. I've brought you ever so far out of your way."

Just then the door of the cottage opened and a little girl about Mary's age came out. She was a pretty little girl with long curly hair, and she had a big sun-bonnet on her head. Her dress reached right to her shoes and her little feet twinkled in and out as she walked.

"I say, Mary, Quite Contrary!" called the little man. "I've made a dreadful mistake. This little girl's name is Mary, and I've brought her to your cottage thinking she lived here – and she doesn't!"

"Dear me," said Mary Contrary, in a soft little voice. "What a pity! Never mind – she had better come in and rest a little while. She shall have dinner with me, and then I'll see that she gets home all right."

Mary was delighted. She liked Mary Contrary very much indeed. It would be lovely to have dinner with her. She said goodbye to the little man who had made the mistake, and he hurried off down the street, with the hen under his arm clucking loudly.

Mary walked into the garden, and the other Mary took her into her spick-and-span cottage. It was so pretty inside – very small, like a doll's house – but quite big enough for the two children.

"It's so hot that I thought of having ice-cream pudding and ginger-beer for dinner today," said Mary Contrary, "I hope that will suit you all right, Mary."

"Oh yes!" said Mary, delighted. "I think that's the nicest dinner I ever heard of!"

Mary Contrary bustled about getting the table laid and Mary Brown helped her. Then they sat down to the largest ice-cream pudding Mary had ever seen – and do you know, they finished it between them! Then they had a bottle of ginger-beer each. It was really lovely.

"This is the village of Nursery Rhyme," said Mary Contrary. "Tom the Piper's Son lives over there – he's a very naughty boy. I don't have much to do with *him*! Next door lives Jack Horner, but he has a very good opinion of himself – he's always saying that he is a very good boy!"

"Yes, I know all about him," said Mary Brown. "Does Humpty-Dumpty live here too?"

"Yes," said Mary Contrary. "But, you know, he's very silly. He's been warned heaps of times not to sit on walls – but he always will. Then he falls off, and as he is a great big egg, he breaks, and there's such a mess to clear up. All the King's horses and all the King's men can't mend him. But he's all right again by the morning – and off he goes to sit on the wall once more!"

"I wish I could see him," said Mary, excited. "This is a lovely place, I think. Does Polly Flinders live here too?"

"Yes, but she's a dirty little girl," said Mary Contrary, wrinkling up her nose in disgust. "She sits among the cinders and spoils all her nice new clothes. There is the Black Sheep here too. He doesn't belong to Bo Peep, though – all *her* sheep are white. She's a silly girl, she's always losing them."

"But they come home all right, don't they?" asked Mary, anxiously.

"Oh yes, and bring their tails behind them," answered Mary Contrary. "Will you have some more ginger-beer? No? Well, now, what about getting you home? I'll walk part of the way with you – and perhaps you wouldn't mind if I gave one of my pretty maids – my dolls, you know – a ride in Josephine's pram for a treat?"

"Of course!" said Mary, getting up and smiling. "I know Josephine would love to have someone in the pram with her."

So Mary Contrary tucked up Esmeralda, her best pretty maid, into the pram beside Josephine, and the two dolls were very happy to be with one another. Mary loved to see her own doll smiling so cheerfully.

Off the two little girls went. Mary looked excitedly at all the little houses she passed. A little girl with a red cloak and hood stood at the door of one and Mary felt sure she was Red Riding Hood. She saw Johnny Thin who put the cat in the well, and Johnny Stout, who pulled him out. She waved to the Old Woman who lived in a shoe, and wished she could go nearer to the funny old house in the shape of a shoe and look at it. But she was afraid that the Old Woman might think she was one of her many children, and put her to bed.

At last they left the strange village behind and went into the wood. It wasn't very long before they were on the right path to Mary's home.

"Well, you know the way now," said Mary Contrary kissing Mary Brown. "Do come and see me again, won't you? And be sure to bring Josephine with you."

She took Esmeralda out of the pram, kissed Josephine goodbye, and stood waving to Mary as she went along the green path. Mary hurried along, anxious to tell her mother all her adventures.

Mother *was* surprised! She couldn't believe her ears!

"Well, you shall come with me next time I go to see Mary Contrary," promised Mary Brown. "I know you'll love to see everybody!"

So her mother is going with her tomorrow. I *do* hope they find the right path, don't you?

The doll that ran away to sea

Lulu had eleven dolls, and she used to sit them in a row on the playroom table every night before she went to bed. There were two fairy dolls, two baby dolls, one walking doll, one French doll with real eyelashes, two wooden Dutch dolls, two little Japanese dolls — and one sailor doll.

Now the sailor doll was a boy doll, and he didn't like being all day long with fairy dolls, baby dolls and others. He said he would rather be with soldiers or teddy bears. He thought the other dolls were silly.

"I ought to belong to a boy!" he said. "I

don't like living with a lot of sillies like you!"

All the dolls thought him very rude, and they told him so.

"You ought to be glad to live in a playroom like this, with a kind owner

who doesn't pull us to pieces!" said the walking doll.

"I want adventures!" said the sailor doll. "I'd like to have a boat of my own, and go to sea! Oh, how brave I'd be! I'd fight pirates and sharks, I'd be wrecked on an island, and make a boat of my own. You don't know how brave I am!"

"No, we don't," said one of the fairy dolls. "But we know who ran away when a spider came on to the table the other night, though!"

The sailor doll went red, and didn't say any more. But that night he made up his mind to run away and go to sea. He knew that there was a stream at the bottom of the garden, and he had seen a little toy boat there, made of paper.

"I'll go right away from these silly dolls," he thought. "I'll sail away tonight and be a daring sailor!"

So that night, when Lulu had sat all her dolls in a row on the table, with the sailor doll in the middle, he got up and said goodbye.

"I'm going!" he told them. "You are a lot of babies, and a sailor like me wants adventures! Goodbye!"

He slid down the tablecloth and went to the window. He climbed up on a chair, and then got on the window-sill. The window was open at the bottom, and the sailor doll slipped out. He jumped on to the grass below, and hurried off down the garden. The moon was just rising, but the garden was full of shadows. Things looked quite different from the daytime.

"Tvit! Tvit!" a loud voice suddenly cried above him, and he jumped in fright. Then a large thing flew close to his head, and the sailor doll was so frightened that he fell flat to the ground.

"Oh, it's only a doll!" said the big brown owl, in disappointment. "I thought it was a mouse."

"Was that horrid thing an owl?" said the doll to himself, and he got up, feeling rather ashamed of himself. He went on down the path, and then gave a yell.

"Ooh! A snake! A great crawly snake!"

"Don't be silly," said the owl, flying low down. "That's a big worm coming out for a night stroll. What a little coward you are!"

"No, I'm not," said the sailor doll, sticking out his chest. "I'm as brave as can be! I'm not a bit afraid!"

Just as he said that, who should come rushing round the corner of the path but Prickles the hedgehog, hurrying to find some beetles for his supper. He bumped right into the sailor doll, who began to howl with pain.

"Ooh, I've walked into a lot of needles! Ooh, I'm being pricked all over! What is it, what is it?"

"What a noise you make, to be sure!" said the hedgehog. "I'm sorry I ran into you, but really, you should look where you're going, you know."

Prickles ran off, and left the doll rubbing all the places in which he had been pricked. Then the doll stuck out his chest again and went on, making up his mind to be really brave, whatever happened.

He had almost got down to the stream when something ran up to him. The sailor doll thought he was going to be bitten, and turned and ran away, full of fear. He heard the patter of footsteps after him, and he ran faster. But the footsteps came faster still, and then he heard a little squeaky voice.

"Please, Mister, stop a minute! Can you tell me the time?"

It was a tiny mouse! Oh dear, how dreadfully ashamed of himself the sailor doll was. He stopped at once, and pretended that he hadn't really been running away at all.

"I haven't a watch," he said. "But if you listen hard, you will hear the church clock striking soon, and then you will know what time it is."

"Thank you," said the little mouse. "You're not very brave, are you? Ho ho, it was funny to see you run away from me!"

The sailor doll didn't answer. He went straight down to the stream, and looked for the paper boat. It was there, drawn up on the bank, all ready to sail. The doll felt very brave. He pushed it out on the water, and got in. Then he gave a shout!

"Ho!" he cried. "I'm a sailor doll, and I'm running away to sea!"

A big frog popped its head out of the water, and then it swam to the paper boat.

"Take me with you!" it cried. "I'll be your crew!"

It put its head over the side of the paper boat, and the sailor doll was in a terrible fright.

"What a horrid-looking monster!" he said. "Go away! Go away!"

"No, I'm coming with you!" said the frog, and it began to climb into the boat.

"I shall be eaten, I know I shall!"

shouted the sailor doll in fear. The frog climbed right into the boat – but it was too heavy for the little paper vessel, which suddenly began to fill with water.

"Oh, it's sinking, it's sinking!" cried the sailor doll. And sure enough in half a minute the little boat had sunk to the bottom. The frog swam off in disgust, and the sailor doll had to scramble to shore as best he could. He was wet through, cold and frightened. He thought of the warm nursery, and his old friends, the dolls, all sitting in a neat row on the table, chatting to each other through the night. How he wished he was back with them!

"I'll go back home!" said the sailor doll, with tears in his eyes. "I'm not a bit brave. I am much sillier than even the baby dolls! I hate adventures!"

He ran off up the garden path, and climbed in at the window again. He hauled himself up the tablecloth and ran to where the dolls all sat in a row.

How surprised they were to see him!

"Oh, you poor thing, you're wet through!" cried the walking doll. "Let me dry you with a piece of the tablecloth."

"We *are* glad to see you back!" said the two fairy dolls. "Couldn't you find the way to go to sea?"

"No," said the sailor doll. "The way is full of dreadful flying dragons, and snakes, and prickly monsters, and the stream is full of things that climb into boats and sink them. Adventures are horrid. I don't want them any more. I am glad to be home with you again."

"Poor old sailor doll!" said everyone. "Never mind, we'll be nice to you!"

So they all settled down together once more, and the sailor doll never said again that he wanted to go to sea.

And wasn't Lulu astonished to find him so wet the next morning! She *couldn't* think what had happened – and the sailor doll was much too ashamed to tell her!

Mother Hubbard's honey

Mother Hubbard kept bees, and they made lovely golden honey for her. Mother Hubbard took it from the hives and put it into jars.

Then her cupboard was full when she went to it, instead of bare. Rows upon rows of honey jars stood there, waiting to be sold.

Now little Pixie Peep-About lived next door to Mother Hubbard, and he loved honey. But he wasn't a very good or very helpful pixie, so Mother Hubbard didn't give him any honey. She sold most of it, gave some to her friends, and kept six pots for herself.

Pixie Peep-About was cross because she never gave him any honey. "And I

live next door, too!" he said to himself. "She might have given me just a taste. She knows I love honey."

But Peep-About never gave Mother Hubbard any of his gooseberries when they were ripe. And he didn't offer her an egg when his hens laid plenty. So it wasn't surprising that he didn't get any honey.

One summer he watched Mother Hubbard's bees.

"How busy they are!" he said, as he peeped over the wall. "In and out, in and out of those hives all the day long. And what is more, a lot of those bees come into *my* garden and take the honey from *my* flowers!"

It was quite true. They did. But bees go anywhere and everywhere, so of course they went into Peep-About's garden too.

"Some of that honey they are storing in Mother Hubbard's hives is mine, taken from my flowers," thought Peep-About. "So Mother Hubbard ought to give me plenty!"

He told Mother Hubbard this, but she laughed. "Honey is free in the flowers!" she said. "Don't be silly, Peep-About."

Now, one day Mother Hubbard went

to take the honeycombs from her hives. They were beautiful combs, full of golden honey. She meant to separate the honey from the combs, and store it in her jars. Peep-About knew she was going to do that. She did it every year.

"Now she'll have jars upon jars of honey, and she won't give me a single one," thought the pixie. "It's too bad. I haven't tasted honey for months, and I should love some on bread and butter."

Mother Hubbard poured the honey into her jars. She handed one to old Mister Potter, at the bottom of the garden. He was a kind old fellow, and always gave Mother Hubbard tomatoes when he had some to spare. He was delighted.

"Look at that now!" said Peep-About to himself. "Not a drop for me! Mean old thing! My, what delicious honey it looked!"

The next day Mother Hubbard

dressed herself up in her best coat and hat, and set out to catch the bus, with three pots of honey in her basket. Peep-About met her as she went to the bus.

"Where are you going?" asked Peep-About.

"To see my sister, Dame Blue-Bonnet," said Mother Hubbard. "I'll be gone all day, so if you see the milkman, Peep-About, tell him to leave me a pint of milk."

"Gone all day!" thought Peep-About. "Well, what about me getting in at the kitchen window, going to that cupboard, and helping myself to a few spoonfuls of honey!"

So, when Mother Hubbard had safely got on the bus, Peep-About crept in at her kitchen window and went to the cupboard. It wasn't locked. He opened it, and saw row upon row of jars of honey. Oh, what a lovely sight!

He was small and the cupboard was high. He tried to scramble up to one of the shelves, and he upset a jar of honey. Down it went, and poured all over him!

"Gracious!" said Peep-About in alarm. "It's all over me! How lovely it tastes!"

He thought he had better go into his own home, scrape the honey off himself, and eat it that way. So out of the window he went.

But the garden was full of Mother Hubbard's bees, and they smelt the honey on Peep-About at once.

"Zzzzzz! Honey! ZZZZZZZ! Honey!" they buzzed to one another, and flew round Peep-About. They tried to settle on the honey that was running down his head and neck.

"Go away! Go away! Stop buzzing round me!" he cried. But no matter how he waved them away, they came back again.

And now Peep-About had a terrible time, for wherever he went the bees went too. They followed him into his kitchen. They stung him when he flapped them away. They followed him out into the garden again. They followed him into the street. They wouldn't leave Peep-About alone for one minute.

He couldn't sit down and have his dinner. He had to go without his tea. He ran here and he ran there, but always the bees flew with him.

He had their honey on him, and they wanted it.

More and more bees came to join in the fun. At last Peep-About saw Mother Hubbard walking up her front path and he ran to her. She was astonished to see her bees round him in a big buzzing cloud.

"Take them away! Make them go to their hive!" wept Peep-About.

Mother Hubbard touched him and found he was sticky with honey. Then she knew what had happened.

"You went to steal some of my honey," she said, sternly. "You're a bad pixie. You can keep the honey — and the bees too! I shan't call them off!"

So, until the bees went to bed in their hive that night, poor Peep-About had to put up with them. He ran for miles trying to get rid of them, but he couldn't. They could fly faster than he could run!

At last the bees went to bed.

Peep-About stripped off his sticky suit and washed it. He got himself a meal. He cried all the time. "I shall never like honey again," he wept. "Never, never, never!"

Mother Hubbard was sorry the next day that she hadn't helped poor Peep-About, even though he had been a bad little pixie. So she sent him a tiny jar of honey all for himself.

But wasn't it a pity – he couldn't eat it! He didn't like honey any more. He couldn't bear to look at it.

"It serves me right!" he said. "When I couldn't have it, I loved it, and tried to take it. Now, here I've got a jar, and I can't bear to eat it. It's a good punishment for me, it really is!"

Mollie's mud-pies

It was very hot, so hot that Mollie wore only a swimsuit. It was nearly summer, and Mummy said if it was so hot now, whatever would it be like in the middle of summer.

"It's nice," said Mollie, who liked wearing almost nothing. She didn't even wear shoes in the garden. "I like it, Mummy. I do wish we were by the sea, then I could swim."

"Well, I'll tell you what I will do," said her mother. "I will water you each night before you go to bed!"

"Water me!" said Mollie, in surprise. "What do you mean, Mummy?"

"Just what I say," said Mummy. "I'll fill a can with half-warm water, and

then water you before you go to bed.
That will be fun for you."

"Oh, *yes*," said Mollie in delight. "I
should love that."

She played in the hot garden. The
grass looked yellow, not green.
Everywhere was dried up and dusty.
Mollie wondered if the birds had any
puddles to drink from. They must be
thirsty now, with all the puddles dried
up. So she filled a little bowl with water,
and set it out on the grass. It was fun to
see the birds coming to drink from it.

"They drink so sweetly," said Mollie.
"They dip in their beaks, and then hold
their heads back, Mummy, and let the
water run down their throats."

When the evening came, Mummy
filled a big watering-can with half-
warm water, and called Mollie. "Come
and have your watering!"

"Will it make me grow, like the
flowers?" cried Mollie, dancing about.
Mummy tipped up the can. Mollie gave
a squeal. Although the water was not

cold, it felt cold on her hot little body. She danced about, squeaking with excitement and joy.

"The water's made a nice muddy patch on the path," she cried. "Look, my toes are brown and muddy with dancing in it."

"You'll have to wash them well," said Mummy, filling the can again. "Come along – one more watering and you must go to bed."

The patch of path was indeed wet and muddy after the second can of water had been poured all over Mollie. "If it's wet tomorrow, I shall make little mud-pies of it," said Mollie.

It was still muddy the next day. After breakfast Mollie went to the mud and dabbled her fingers in it. "I shall make little pies and cakes of mud, and set them in the sun to dry," she thought. "That will be a nice game to play."

Mummy called her. "If you want to play that dirty game you must wear an overall over that nice clean swimsuit. Come along."

Mollie ran indoors. When she came out again she found someone else in her mud-patch! It was a little bird with a touch of white at the foot of his dark, long tail, and underneath his body. He stared at Mollie, and then scraped up some mud in his beak.

"Oh!" said Mollie, pleased. "Are you making mud-pies too? I never knew a bird liked playing with mud before. Do play with me."

The little bird gave a twitter, filled his beak quite full, and then suddenly darted into the air on curving wings.

Mollie saw that he had a forked tail behind him.

"I wish he hadn't gone," she thought. "It would have been fun to play with him. I suppose he has taken the mud to make mud-pies somewhere else."

Suddenly the little bird came back again. He looked at Mollie, and she looked at him. He wondered if Mollie was the kind of child to throw stones at him, or to shout and frighten him away.

But she wasn't. She was like you. She liked birds, and wanted them to stay close to her so that she could watch them and make friends with them.

She sat quite still and watched him. He went to the mud again, and began to scrape up some more. Then another bird, exactly like him, flew down, and he began to dabble in it as well. Mollie was delighted.

"Everyone is making mud-pies this morning," she said. "Gracious – here's another! How busy they all are in my muddy patch. I'll get busy too."

Once the birds had made up their minds that Mollie was a friend, they became very busy indeed. They filled their little beaks with mud time after time, and then flew away round the house. Mollie wondered where they went. They kept coming and going all the morning.

"Funny little mud-pie birds," she said to them. "Do you bake your mud-pies up on the roof somewhere? I bake mine here, look!"

The hot sun baked her pies beautifully. She put them on a plate out of her tea-set and took them in to her mummy.

"Have a mud-pie?" she said. "They are lovely. And, oh, Mummy, the mud-pie birds have played in the mud with me all morning. They were sweet."

Mummy was surprised. "Mud-pie birds! Whatever do you mean?"

"Well, they came and played with my mud and took some away to make mud-pies with. I expect they baked them up on the roof," said Mollie.

Mummy thought it was a little tale of Mollie's. She pretended to eat Mollie's mud-pie, and then offered Mollie a bun from the oven.

"I've been baking too," she said. "Have a hot bun? And now I think you had better stop playing with the mud and wash yourself."

"The mud is gone now," said Mollie. "The sun has baked it hard."

The little birds didn't come into the garden any more that day. "I suppose they only came for the mud," thought Mollie. "Well, if Mummy waters me again tonight there will be more mud tomorrow for us all to play with."

There was – a nice big patch – and down came the little birds again, to scrape up the mud. Mollie was so pleased.

"It's nice to have you to play with me," she said to the busy little birds. "But I really wish you would tell me what you do with your mud."

They twittered a little song to her, high and sweet, but she didn't understand what they said. They flew to and from the mud all morning, till the sun dried it up.

"Mummy, why do the mud-pie birds take my mud?" asked Mollie. "I do want to know. I didn't know that birds like mud so much."

Her daddy was there, and he looked up from his newspaper. "What's all this about mud-pie birds?" he asked. So Mollie told him.

"Ah," he said. "Now I know what birds you mean. Your mud-pie birds are house-martins, cousins of the pretty swallows we see flying high in the air all summer."

"House-martins!" said Mollie. "I should call them mud-martins. What do they do with my mud?"

"Come with me and I'll show you," said Daddy. He took Mollie's hand, and led her upstairs. They went into her

bedroom. Daddy went to the window and opened it wide.

"Now look out of your window, above it, to the edge of the roof overhead," he said. "Tell me what you see."

Mollie leaned out, and looked up. She gave a cry. "Oh, Daddy! The mud-pie birds are there. They are making something of my mud. What is it?"

"It's a nest," said Daddy. "The house-martins don't use dead leaves and twigs and moss for their nests as most birds do. They make them of mud. They fetch beakfuls of mud, and plaster it against the wall, gradually building it out till they have made a fine nest of mud, with a hole to get in and out. There's the hole in that nest. Look!"

As Mollie watched, one of the little birds flew up with his beak full of mud from somewhere, and pressed it against the edge of his nest.

"There you are," said Daddy. "He brings wet mud, and it dries hard in the sun, making a perfectly good nest for his little wife to lay her eggs in, and have her young ones."

"Oh, Daddy! Fancy making a nest of my mud, the mud that was made when Mummy watered me each evening," said Mollie in delight. "I couldn't think why the mud-birds came to make mud-pies. I did not know they were making mud-nests – and over my bedroom window, too, tucked under the edge of the roof! I shall hear them calling and twittering to each other all day long. Look – there's another nest farther along. You won't pull them down, will you?"

"Of course not!" said Daddy, who was fond of birds. "They can nest there in peace and happiness, out of reach of the cats. Later on we shall see their young ones popping their heads out of the holes in the mud-nests."

And so they did! The house-martins laid eggs in their strange mud-nests, and in a few weeks' time Mollie saw three or four tiny feathery heads popping out of the hole in the nest above her window, waiting for the father and mother to come back with flies to feed them.

Later still the little birds flew into the sky with their mother and father, learning how to dart and soar and glide, and how to catch the hundreds of insects that flew in the air. Daddy said they did a great deal of good, because the flies were a pest.

And then one day they were all gone. Mollie looked into the sky and they were not there.

"They've gone away south, where it

is warmer," said Daddy. "There will be plenty of insects for them to eat there. Our winter is coming and they do not like that."

"I don't want them to go away," said Mollie sadly.

"Well, they will be back again in the spring," said Daddy. "And, Mollie, if the weather is hot and dry again when they come back, you must make a muddy patch once more, and they will come to it, and build their nest again over your window. They love to come back to exactly the same place, if they can."

So, of course, Mollie is going to watch for them when the spring comes. You must watch too, and if we have hot and dry weather in May, when the mud-pie birds want to build their nests, you can do as Mollie did – make a muddy patch for them, and watch them fly down to it to fill their beaks.

Maybe they will build a mud-nest over your window, too. That really would be fun, wouldn't it?

She was always at the bottom

Janie did her very best at school, but no matter how she tried, she always was at the bottom of her class. Wasn't it a pity?

She wasn't any good at sums, and her writing was rather like spiders'

103

legs running over the page. She found it very difficult to read, and she couldn't sing in tune.

But Mummy didn't really mind. "I know you do your best, darling," she often said to Janie. "That's all that matters."

Janie didn't worry for herself – she was only sorry because, when the prize-giving day came, she never had a prize and couldn't make her mother proud of her. She saw all the other children proudly going up to the platform to get prizes for sums, writing, and reading, but Janie had to sit still in her seat, for there was never a prize for her.

Once her mummy found her crying about it, and she put her arm round her to comfort her.

"Janie, you may not be the cleverest girl in the school, you may not be the hardest-working girl – but there is something you *can* be, if you try."

"What's that, Mummy?" asked Janie, wiping her eyes.

"You can be the kindest girl!" said Mummy. "What about trying that, Janie? I shall be very proud of you, then. A great many boys and girls can be clever – but it isn't everyone that is kind."

Well, Janie thought she would try. So she began. She sharpened Donald's pencils for him. She broke her rubber in half and gave a piece to Gladys when she had lost hers. She shared her biscuits with George when he had forgotten his one morning.

She brought Miss Brown some flowers from her own little garden at home. She offered to take home the caterpillars each weekend to look after them for the class – and she looked after them well, too.

"Really, Janie, you're a very helpful girl," Miss Brown said. "You were bottom of the class again this week, but for helpfulness I really think you are at the top!"

Janie was pleased! She found that

the other children liked her more and more, because she was always kind and generous to them. If the little ones fell down and hurt their knees, it was always Janie they went to, to be bandaged. If anybody trapped their fingers in desks or doors, they would run to Janie at once.

Soon the end of the term came along as usual. The children began to talk about exams and marks and prizes.

"I shall be top in maths!" said George proudly. "I was last year, too."

"And I'm sure I shall get the writing prize," said Ellen. "I hope it's a book. I love reading."

"Miss Brown says if I work as hard as I have been doing all the term I shall have the reading prize," said Donald, who was a wonderful reader.

Janie listened and said nothing. There wasn't anything she could get a prize for, she knew. The children looked at her. Last year they had laughed at Janie because she was the dunce, and didn't get any prizes at all. But this year they didn't laugh.

"You know, I do so like Janie," said Ellen to Donald. "I'm sorry she won't get a prize. It must be horrid for her to sit beside her mother whilst we go up and collect our prizes. Other people who don't get prizes this year probably got them last year – but Janie never gets one any year!"

Well, all the children got together in a corner of the playground one morning and had a talk about Janie. Janie couldn't imagine what they were talking about! They wouldn't let her come near them, and she felt rather hurt.

"Oh dear! Why are they leaving me out?" she thought. "This is horrid!"

But the children were not really being horrid. They were planning a nice surprise for Janie!

"Do let's all bring a penny or two and ask Miss Brown to buy a prize for Janie!" they were saying.

"But whatever shall we give her a prize for?" wondered Alice. "She isn't really good at anything, not even games or needlework."

"Well, she's jolly good at being kind," said George. "Let's say it's a prize for kindness."

Well, after they had planned this, they went to Miss Brown. Still they wouldn't let Janie into their secret and the little girl went home in tears. She couldn't understand why she was being left out of the children's secrets so suddenly.

Miss Brown thought it was a splendid idea. She smiled at the children. "Bring your pennies," she said, "and I will count them and see what we can buy."

So, very secretly, each child brought five pence or ten pence, and some even brought twenty pence. They gave the money to Miss Brown and she counted it all up.

"There is quite a lot," she said. "One pound and twenty-five pence! What shall we buy for Janie's prize?"

"She won't want a book," said Donald. "She doesn't read well enough, and she's not fond of games like snap or ludo. But, Miss Brown, she does love dolls."

"Well, what about a doll?" said Miss Brown. "Alice, you come with me this afternoon and look in the toyshop to see what sort of dolls they have."

So Alice and Miss Brown looked in the toyshop that afternoon – and there they saw a lovely baby doll, dressed in a woolly dress and jacket, smiling at them.

"That's just what Janie would like!" cried Alice. "But, oh dear – it's one pound and seventy-five pence! I can give ten pence more of my money towards the price, Miss Brown, but that's all I've got."

"Well, I will give the extra forty pence," said Miss Brown. "So the prize will be from me, too. Come along into the shop and we'll buy the doll."

In they went – and the baby doll was

soon packed into a long box with tissue-paper round her face. Alice proudly carried the box back to school, and that afternoon she showed the children Janie's prize. Even the boys liked the doll.

"It looks such a smiley doll," said George.

Janie had been sent home first by Miss Brown. She wondered why. Really, everyone seemed to be keeping her out of their secrets lately. It was too bad!

"Mummy, it's the prize-giving day tomorrow," she told her mother when the day came near. "You won't be very proud of me again, I'm afraid, because I'm bottom in all the exams. But I've got to go tomorrow afternoon. Would you like to come, or do you think it will be a waste of time for you when you have a little girl who never wins anything?"

"Of course I'll come," said Mummy at once. "There is going to be singing and reciting too, isn't there, Janie? I'd love to hear that."

"Yes, but I'm not in anything much," said Janie sadly. "And lately the children have been having secrets and not telling me, Mummy. So it hasn't been much good me trying to be kind, as you said."

"It's always worthwhile being kind," said Mummy. "Don't stop, Janie. Just go on, please."

Well, the prize-giving afternoon came at last. The children sang and recited. The headmistress made a speech. Miss Brown said a few words too. All the parents clapped and cheered.

Then the prizes were given out. One by one the children went up to the platform and took their books, games, and toys. They were so proud. Their mothers clapped them loudly, feeling very pleased indeed. Janie's mother clapped all the other children too, and so did Janie.

And then came the surprise of the afternoon. Miss Brown got up and went to the front, when only one prize remained to be given.

"And now," she said, "I have a very special prize, given for a very special thing. This prize is given by all the children and by me, too – not for any lessons or games or handiwork – but for kindness. Janie White, you may not be top of lessons – but you *are* top in kindness! Please come up and get your prize!"

Janie simply couldn't believe her ears! Why, she had won a prize – a real prize for herself, at last! And a prize for kindness, too! The little girl went as red as a beetroot, and stood up to go to the platform. Her mother was so surprised and delighted that she almost forgot to clap Janie!

And you should have heard the clapping and cheering when Janie went up to get her prize! It was far louder and much longer than it had been for anyone else.

"Three cheers for our Janie!" yelled Donald. "Hip, hip, hurrah!"

Miss Brown patted Janie on the shoulder. The headmistress smiled at her. Janie took her big box and walked back to her mother, prouder than she had ever been in her life. When she undid the box and saw the doll smiling up at her, she was so pleased that she danced round her seat in joy.

She took the doll home. She got ready a cot for it. She bathed it and put a night-dress on its fat little body. She was very happy indeed.

"Janie," said her mother, "I would far rather you had a prize for kindness than for any lesson. I am VERY proud of you."

"I know now why the children were having secrets," said Janie. "They were planning my prize! Oh, Mummy, let's give a party for my new doll and ask all the children to it. Wouldn't it be fun?"

Well, the party is tomorrow, and the doll has a new frock for it. All the children are going – I expect you'd like to go too, if you could, wouldn't you?

Conceited Clara

C lara was a doll – and goodness, what a marvellous doll she was! She wore a blue silk dress, a wonderful coat to match, blue shoes and socks, and a hat that was so full of flowers it looked like a little garden.

It was the hat that everyone admired so much. There were daisies, buttercups, cornflowers, poppies and grass round the hat, and it suited Clara perfectly. She knew this, so she always wore her hat, even when she played games with the toys.

"You are vain, Clara!" said the teddy bear teasingly.

That made Clara go red. She *was* vain, and she knew she was pretty.

She knew that her clothes were lovely. She knew that her flowery hat was the prettiest one the toys had ever seen, and that it made her look really sweet.

"I'm not vain!" said Clara. "Not a bit!"

"You are! You're conceited and stuck-up," said the teddy bear, who always said what he thought. "You even wear

your hat when you play with us. And if we play a bit roughly you turn up your nose and say, 'Oh, please! You'll tear my pretty frock!' Pooh! Conceited Clara!"

Clara was angry. She glared at the bear and then she walked straight up to him. She took hold of his pink bow and tugged at it. It came undone, and Clara pulled it off. And then she tore the ribbon in half. Wasn't she naughty?

"Oh! You horrid doll! Look what you've done! You've torn my ribbon and now I can't tie it round my neck, and I shall show where my head is sewn on to my body," wept the bear.

"Serves you right," said Clara, and she walked off.

Well, after that the toys wouldn't have anything to do with Clara. They wouldn't play with her. They wouldn't talk to her. They wouldn't even speak when she called to them. So Clara was cross and unhappy.

One night, when the children were asleep and the toys came alive to play, Clara took her beautiful flowery hat and hung it up in the dolls' house. She thought perhaps the toys might play with her if she didn't wear her hat. She fluffed out her curly hair and gazed at the teddy bear.

"Ho!" said the bear. "Now you want to show off your curly hair, I suppose! Well, go and show it somewhere else! *We* don't want to see it, Conceited Clara!"

So that wasn't any use. Clara went to a corner and sulked. She was very angry. How dare the toys take no notice of her, the prettiest doll in the whole nursery!

Then the toys planned a party. It was the birthday of the clockwork mouse, and everyone loved him because he was such a dear. So they thought they would have a party for him and games, and give him a lovely time.

But they didn't ask Clara. The teddy

cooked some exciting cakes and biscuits on the stove in the dolls' house, and cut up a rosy apple into slices. The toys set out the chairs round the little wooden table and put the dishes and plates ready.

Everything looked so nice. "It's a pity that we can't put a vase of flowers in the middle of the table," said the teddy bear. "I always think flowers look so sweet at a party. Come along, everyone – we'll just go and tidy ourselves up and then the party can begin."

They all went to find the brush and comb in the toy-cupboard. Clara peeped from her corner and thought that the birthday-table looked lovely with its cakes and biscuits and apple-slices.

"I do wish I had something to give the clockwork mouse," thought Clara. "I do love him. He's such a dear. But I expect he would throw it back at me if I had anything to give. The toys are all so horrid to me now."

And then Clara suddenly had a

marvellous idea. What about her flowery hat? Couldn't she take the flowers off that beautiful hat and put them into a vase for the middle of the birthday-table? They would look really lovely.

She rushed to get her hat. She tore the flowers from it. She found a dear little vase, and began to put them in – buttercups, daisies, cornflowers, poppies and grass. You can't think how sweet they looked.

Clara popped the vase of flowers in the middle of the table and went back to her corner. She looked at her hat rather sadly. It looked very odd without its flowers. She would look funny if she wore it any more.

The toys ran to the birthday-table to begin the party – and how they stared when they saw the lovely flowers in the middle of the table!

"Where did they come from?" cried the teddy bear in astonishment.

"Oh, what a lovely surprise for me!"

cried the clockwork mouse. And then he guessed who had put the flowers there for him.

"It's Clara! They are the flowers out of her hat!" he squeaked. "Oh, Clara, thank you! Do, do come to my party!"

"Yes, do come!" cried all the toys. And the bear ran and took her hand.

"If you can give up the flowers you were so proud of, you can't be so horrid after all!" he cried. "Come along, Clara, and join the party."

So Clara went, and everyone was so nice to her that she was quite happy again. Sometimes she wears her hat without the flowers, and do you know what the toys say? They say, "Why, Clara, you look just as nice without the flowers – you really do!"

And so she does!

Millicent Mary's surprise

Once there was a little girl called Millicent Mary. She had a dear little garden of her own, and in the early spring the very first things that came up were the white snowdrops.

Millicent Mary loved them. She loved the straight green stalks that came up, holding the white bud tightly wrapped up at the top. She liked the two green leaves that sprang up each side. She loved to see the bud slowly unwrap itself, and hang down like a little bell.

But she was always very disappointed because the white bells didn't ring.

"They ought to," said Millicent Mary, and she shook each snowdrop to see if she could make it ring. "Bells like this should ring – they really should! Ring, little snowdrop, ring!"

But not one would ring. Still, Millicent Mary wouldn't give it up. Every morning when she put on her hat and coat and went into the garden, she bent down and shook the snowdrops to see if perhaps today they would say ting-a-ling-a-ling. But they never did.

One day she went to her garden when the snow was on the ground. The snowdrops were buried beneath the snow, and Millicent Mary had to scrape the white snow away very gently to find out where her snowdrops were.

At last all the little white bells were showing. She shook them but no sound came. "Well, you might have rung just a tiny tune to tell me you were grateful to me for scraping the snow away!" said Millicent Mary.

She was just going to stand up and go to the shed to fetch her broom when she saw something rather strange. The snow on the bed nearby seemed to be moving itself – poking itself up as if something was underneath it, wriggling hard.

Millicent Mary was surprised. She was even more surprised when she heard a very tiny voice crying, "Help me! Oh, help me!"

"Goodness gracious!" said the little girl. "There's something buried under the snow just there – and it's got a little tiny voice that speaks!"

She began to scrape away the snow, and her soft, gentle fingers found something small and strange under the white blanket. She pulled out – well, guess what she pulled out!

Yes – you guessed right. It was a tiny pixie, a fairy with frozen silver wings and a little shivering body dressed in a cobweb dress.

"Oh, thank you!" said the pixie in a tiny voice, like a bird cheeping. "I was so tired last night that I crept under a dead leaf and fell asleep. And when I awoke this morning I found a great, thick, cold, white blanket all over me – and I couldn't get it off! Just wait till I catch the person who threw this big blanket all over the garden!"

Millicent Mary laughed. "It's snow!" she said. "It isn't a real blanket. You poor little thing, you feel so cold, you are freezing my fingers. I'm going to take you indoors and get you warm."

She tucked the pixie into her pocket and went indoors. She didn't think she would show the fairy to anyone, because she might vanish – and Millicent Mary didn't want her to do that. It was fun having a pixie, not as big as a doll, to warm before the fire!

The pixie sat on the fender and stretched out her frozen toes to the dancing flames. Millicent Mary took a piece of blue silk out of her mother's rag-bag and gave it to the pixie.

"Wrap this round you for a cloak," she said. "It will keep out the frost when you leave me."

The pixie was delighted. She wrapped
the bit of blue silk all round her
and pulled it close. "I shall get my
needle and thread and make this
lovely piece of silk into a proper coat
with sleeves and buttons and collar,"
she said. "You are a dear little girl!
I love you. Yes, really I do. Is there
anything you would like me to give
you?"

Millicent Mary thought hard. Then
she shook her head. "No," she said at

last. "There isn't anything at all, really. I've got all the toys I want. I did badly want a dolls' house, but I had one for Christmas. I don't want any sweets because I've got a tin of barley-sugar. I don't want chocolate biscuits because Mummy bought some yesterday. No – I can't think of anything."

The pixie looked most disappointed. "I do wish you'd try to think of something," she said. "Try hard!"

Millicent Mary thought again. Then she smiled. "Well," she said, "there *is* something I'd simply love – but it needs magic to do it, I think. I'd *love* it if my snowdrops could ring on my birthday, which is on February 13th!"

"Oh, that's easily managed!" said the pixie. "I'll work a spell for it. Let me see – what's your name?"

"Millicent Mary," said the little girl.

"Millicent Mary," said the pixie, writing it down in a tiny notebook. "Birthday, 13th February. Wants snowdrops to ring on that day. All right – I'll see to it! And now goodbye, my dear. I'm deliciously warm with this blue silk. See you again some day. Don't forget to listen to your snowdrops on February 13th!"

She skipped up into the air, spread her silvery wings, and flew straight out of the top of the window. Millicent Mary couldn't help feeling tremendously excited. Her birthday would soon be here – and just imagine the snowdrops ringing!

Won't she love to shake each tiny white bell, and hear it ring ting-a-ling-a-ling, ting-a-ling-a-ling! Is *your* name Millicent Mary, by any chance, and is *your* birthday on 13th February? If it is, the snowdrops will ring for you too, without a doubt – so don't forget to shake each little white bell on that day, and hear the tinkling sound they make. What a lovely surprise for all the Millicent Marys!

The empty dolls' house

Sally had a lovely little dolls' house on Christmas Day. She looked at it standing there at the foot of her bed. It had a little blue front door with a tiny knocker that really knocked, and it had four small windows, with tiny lace curtains at each!

"Oh, it's lovely!" said Sally. "Won't my little Belinda Jane love to live there! She is small enough to fit it properly."

But when she opened the front of the dolls' house, Sally got rather a shock. It was empty. There was no furniture at all!

She was disappointed. A dolls' house can't be played with unless it has furniture inside, and Sally badly wanted to play with it.

Also, Belinda Jane couldn't possibly live there if it was empty. She must at least have a bed to sleep in, a chair to sit on, and a table to have meals on.

She showed the house to Belinda Jane. Belinda looked sad when she saw that it was empty.

"Never mind. I'll save up my money and buy some furniture," said Sally. "Maybe I'll get some money today for a present."

But she didn't. All her aunts and

uncles gave her Christmas presents of toys and books, and nobody gave her any money at all.

It was Granny who had given her the dear little dolls' house. When she came to share Christmas dinner she spoke to Sally about the house.

"I didn't put any furniture in it, dear," she said, "because I thought you would find it more fun to buy some yourself and furnish it bit by bit."

"Yes. It *will* be fun to do that," said Sally. "Only it will take such a long time, Granny, because I spent all my money on Christmas presents, and I only get fifty pence a week, you know."

When Sally got her first fifty pence she went to the toyshop and looked at the dolls' furniture there. She saw a cardboard box, and in it was a dear little bed that would just fit Belinda Jane, two chairs, a table and a wardrobe! Think of that!

But, oh dear, it cost three pounds, and

there was nothing at all that fifty pence would buy! Sally ran home almost in tears!

"Now don't be a baby," said Mummy. "Everything comes to those who wait patiently. Don't get cross and upset if you can't have what you want. It will come!"

Sally was not a very patient person, and she hated waiting for things she badly wanted. But she always believed what Mummy said, so she went up to the playroom and told Belinda Jane they must both be patient, and maybe they would get the furniture somehow in the end.

Sally was excited next day, because she was going to a party – and there was to be a Christmas tree. It was sure to be a nice big one, with a present for everyone. And there would be games and balloons and crackers and ice-creams. Lovely!

She went to the party in her best blue dress. "Hallo, Sally!" cried Eileen, dancing up to her. "There's going to be a prize for every game, did you know? And it's to be money! I do hope I win a prize, because it's Mummy's birthday next week, and I want to buy her some flowers."

Sally was pleased to hear about the prizes, too. If only she could win some of the money! She would be able to buy some furniture for Belinda Jane.

They played musical chairs – but Sally didn't win because a rough little boy pushed her out of her chair, and she didn't like to push back.

They played hunt the thimble, but somehow Sally never could see the thimble first! And when they played spin the tray she couldn't get there before the little spinning tray had fallen over flat! So she didn't win any prizes at all.

"Now, I mustn't get cross or upset," she said to herself. "I mustn't. I must be patient. But I've missed my chance.

What a pity!"

After tea the children were taken into another room – and there was the Christmas tree, reaching up to the ceiling, hung with presents from top to bottom.

Just about the middle of the tree there hung a cardboard box – the cardboard box of furniture that Sally had seen in the toyshop! Her heart jumped for joy. Now surely her patience would have its reward – surely she would get that lovely box of dolls' furniture!

She could hardly wait for the presents to be given out. She had good manners, so she didn't like to ask for the box of furniture. She just stood near by, hoping it would be hers.

But to her very great disappointment, it wasn't given to her! She was handed a box with tiny cars in it instead. Sally could have cried! She said, "Thank you," and went to a corner, trying not to feel upset.

"I wanted to win a prize and I didn't. And I wanted to have the furniture off the tree and I didn't," she thought. "What's the good of being patient? I don't get what I want, however good and patient I am. I feel like shouting and stamping!"

But she didn't shout or stamp, of course, because she knew better. She just sat and looked at the little cars, and didn't like them a bit.

A small girl called Fanny came up to her. She held the box of furniture in her hand. She sat down beside Sally and looked at the tiny cars.

"Oh, aren't they lovely?" she said. "I do like them so much. I got this dolls' furniture, look. Isn't it silly?"

"Well, I think it's lovely," said Sally. "How *can* you think it's silly?"

"It's silly for me, because I haven't got a dolls' house," said Fanny. "But I *have* got a toy garage! I had it for Christmas. It's only got one car in, and I do want some more. That's why I like

THE EMPTY DOLLS' HOUSE

your present and hate mine!"

"Well, *I* had a dolls' house for Christmas without any furniture – and I haven't got a garage!" said Sally, her face very bright. "Can't you give me the furniture and I'll give you the cars? We could ask Eileen's mother, and see if she minds. It was she who bought all the presents for us."

They ran to Eileen's mother, and told her. She smiled at them. "Of course, change your presents if you want to," she said. "I think it would be most sensible of you. I should have given *you* the furniture, Sally, and *you* the cars, Fanny, if I'd known about the dolls' house and the garage."

The little girls were so pleased. Fanny took her cars home to her toy garage and Sally raced home with her dolls' furniture. It went into the dolls' house and looked most beautiful!

"There you are, Belinda Jane," said Sally to her smallest doll. "Now you can move in. You've got a bed to sleep in,

chairs to sit on, a wardrobe for your clothes and a table to have meals on. And I'll buy you a little cooker as soon as ever I can."

Belinda Jane was pleased. She looked sweet sitting on one of the chairs, and even sweeter tucked up in the little bed.

Mummy came to look. Sally gave her a hug. "Mummy, you were right about waiting patiently. I kept *on* being disappointed, but I wouldn't get cross or upset – and then suddenly the furniture just came to me. Wasn't it lucky?"

"It was," said Mummy. "Now, tomorrow I'll give you some old bits-and-pieces and you can make carpets for Belinda Jane. She will like that."

You should see Sally's dolls' house now. She saved up her money and bought a little lamp, a cooker, another bed, a cupboard for the kitchen, two more chairs and a dressing table. I really wouldn't mind living in that dolls' house myself!

She couldn't keep a secret

It wasn't a bit of good telling anything to Marybelle if you wanted to keep it secret – because Marybelle would at once go round and tell everyone else!

It was most annoying. When Kitty told Marybelle she was making a hanky-case for her friend Lucy, and it was to be a real surprise, what did Marybelle do but go and whisper it into Lucy's ear at once. So it wasn't a surprise after all.

And when Tom mentioned to Marybelle that his mother couldn't give him money that week to buy the toy he wanted, Marybelle ran round and told everyone that Tom's mother was so poor she couldn't even buy him a toy!

That made Tom very angry. He spoke to the others when Marybelle wasn't there. "Can't we stop that silly Marybelle from repeating everything, and sometimes repeating it wrong?" he said. "She really does make such mischief – and she never gets punished for it!"

"Well, it's our own fault for telling her things," said Lucy.

"Yes, but you can't remember not to talk to Marybelle," said Tom. "I can't, anyway."

"I think I know how we could stop her running round and repeating everything," said Ronnie, with a grin.

"How?" asked everyone at once.

"Well," said Ronnie, "we could tell her silly, ridiculous things and beg her not to repeat them in case they aren't true – which they wouldn't be, of course. And then when she *does* go and repeat them everyone will laugh at her. She won't like that."

"What kind of things would we say to

her?" asked Tom.

"Well – I could say, 'Marybelle, have you heard that the postman lost all his letters in the duck-pond yesterday?' " said Ronnie. "And I would say, 'Now, don't tell anyone, because it probably isn't true.' But off she would go, of course, and what a to-do there would be!"

"Yes. That sounds a good idea," said Tom. "We'll do it. You tell her that one about the postman to start with, Ronnie."

So Ronnie did. He waited until he had got Marybelle alone, and then he whispered mysteriously to her, "Marybelle, have you heard that the postman lost all his letters in the duck-pond yesterday? Don't repeat it, for it may not be true."

Marybelle's eyes almost fell out of her head. Gracious! All the letters lost – in the duck-pond too!

She ran off at once. "Did you know that the postman dropped all the letters into the duck-pond yesterday?" she said to everyone she met. "Well, he did!"

Now, the postman's little boy heard that Marybelle was saying this, and he asked his father about it. The postman was most annoyed. He went straight to Marybelle's house to see her mother.

"Will you please stop your little girl from saying that I dropped all the letters into the duck-pond yesterday?" he said. "I am most annoyed about it. I have never lost a letter in my life!"

Poor Marybelle! She had to apologize to the postman. She scolded Ronnie for saying such a thing.

"Well, I told you not to repeat it in case it wasn't true," said Ronnie. "It's your own fault."

Now the next day Tom went up to Marybelle and whispered something to her. "Have you heard that old Mrs Loo, the sweetshop woman, gives peppermints to her hens, and that's why she never has any when we want to buy them?" he said. "Now, don't you repeat that, Marybelle, in case it isn't true."

"Gives peppermints to hens!" cried Marybelle. "The silly old woman! No wonder she has none to sell."

Off ran Marybelle to tell everyone. How they laughed at her behind her back! But somebody happened to tell old Mrs Loo about it and she was very cross. And the next time Marybelle went into her shop for some sweets, she wouldn't sell her any.

"No," she said. "You're the silly girl that says I feed my hens with peppermints. Such a stupid thing to say! I'd make them ill if I did. You go away and buy sweets somewhere else."

Marybelle cried. She went to Tom and told him he was mean to tell her something that wasn't true. "Well, I warned you not to say anything, in case it wasn't true," said Tom. "It is your own fault, Marybelle."

Then Lucy had a turn. She went to Marybelle, looking most mysterious.

"Marybelle! Have you heard that the grocer has a pony he will let children ride up and down the street for a penny? Isn't it exciting? But don't say a word about it, in case it isn't true."

Well, Marybelle loved riding ponies, and she made up her mind to be the first one riding the grocer's. So she took a penny from her money-box and ran to the shop.

"Please," she said to the grocer, "here is my penny. Now let me ride on your pony."

"What pony?" said the grocer.

"*Yours!*" said Marybelle. "I've heard that we can ride it for a penny."

"Don't be silly," said the grocer. "I've got no pony, and I wouldn't let you children ride it if I had. Run away and don't come to me with silly ideas like that."

How everyone laughed at Marybelle! She was very angry with Lucy. "Well, I told you it might not be true," said Lucy. "I did warn you, Marybelle."

Then Jack went to Marybelle, and told her a little story of his own. "Marybelle! Have you heard that Teacher's dog chased Mrs Brown's cat, and bit its tail?" he said. "Now, don't you repeat that, in case it isn't true."

Any bit of news, however silly or small, was enough to set Marybelle's tongue wagging. In a trice she was telling everyone what Jack had said.

"I say, did you know that Teacher's dog chased Mrs Brown's cat and bit its tail? Fancy that! Teacher always says her dog never chases cats."

Now, old Mrs Brown was the great-aunt of one of the children. This child told Mrs Brown what Marybelle had said, and she was full of horror to think that her poor cat had been chased and bitten by the teacher's big dog.

So up she went to the school to complain. "I shall go to the police about it if your dog chases my cat again," she said. "A great big dog like that!"

"But he *never* chases anything!" said the teacher, in surprise. "He's too old. Who told you that, Mrs Brown?"

"My great-niece, young Gladys," said Mrs Brown. So Gladys was sent for, and asked about the tale of the dog and cat.

"Oh, Marybelle told me," said Gladys. "She was telling everyone."

Marybelle was sent for, and was scolded by the teacher for saying such an unkind thing about her poor old dog.

"Jack told me," wept Marybelle.

"It was only a made-up story," said Jack, grinning. "I warned Marybelle not to repeat it in case it wasn't true. But she can't help repeating anything, however silly it is – or however secret. We've been telling her all sorts of silly tales, and she's been repeating them all – and getting into trouble, too!"

Marybelle burst into tears again. "You horrid boy! You've got me into trouble."

"No. You got yourself into trouble," said Jack. "And you always will,

Marybelle. You can't hold your tongue, you see, and you can never keep a secret, even if it belongs to somebody else."

"Then I shan't ever believe anything anyone says!" said Marybelle, angrily.

"Right," said Jack. "Then, maybe, you won't repeat it!"

And now poor Marybelle is in a great fix, because she never knows whether any bit of news is true or made-up. So she doesn't dare to repeat it in case she gets into trouble again.

It's a funny way of learning to keep secrets, isn't it? But it's the only way with Marybelles!

The bonnet dame

O nce upon a time, I couldn't tell you how long ago, there lived a strange old woman, who was half a witch. She was always called the bonnet dame, because she got her living by making little white bonnets for babies.

Now the strange thing about Dame Bonnet was that the older she got, the smaller she grew. She was thin and brown, like a bent twig, and her voice was as husky as two leaves rubbing one against the other, but her hands were still as nimble as ever, and she made her white bonnets even more beautifully.

But of course, as she grew smaller, so did the bonnets she made, and after a while mothers didn't buy them any more, for they didn't fit their babies. Then Dame Bonnet went to Brownie-Town and lived there, for the brownies had nice small babies, and her bonnets fitted them well.

Then she grew smaller still and her bonnets no longer fitted even the brownie babies. So she went to Elf-land and there her bonnets fitted the grown-up elves, for they are small creatures, and when Dame Bonnet grew even smaller it didn't matter because then her lovely bonnets fitted the elf babies. So she stayed there quite a long time and was very happy indeed.

Then she grew so very small that the bonnets fitted nobody at all. She tried here and she tried there – the gnomes were far too big in the head; the goblins were the wrong shape, and even the very smallest dwarfs were too large about the head. So Dame Bonnet made no money at all, and began to shrivel away like a dead leaf.

Then one day she met some tiny creatures, slim and sweet, dressed in green. Their heads were bare, and the wind blew their hair about untidily. Dame Bonnet looked at them and wondered if her white bonnets would fit them.

"Who are you?" she asked. "I don't think I've seen you before."

"We are the little Fair Maids," said the small creatures, "half-fairies, half-flowers. We live in the woods, and we are always trying to find a sheltered spot, because the wind blows our hair about so much. He is very rough with us, and we do not like him."

The wind swept down and whipped the tiny creatures' hair about their gentle faces. Dame Bonnet watched, and then she offered them her small white bonnets – so small now that the stitches in them could not be seen!

"Wear these!" she said, in her husky voice. "You need not pay me. Only let me keep near to you, Fair Maids, and

talk to me sometimes. I am an old, old woman, and I would so much like your youthful company to cheer me."

The Fair Maids tried on the small white bonnets, and to their great delight they fitted most beautifully. "Thank you!" they said gratefully. "Please do keep near us if you like, Dame Bonnet. We shall love to talk to you."

Well, my dears, the Fair Maids still wear the tiny white bonnets made by the old half-witch. You can see them any day in February in gardens and woods, half-fairies, half-flowers – small, fairy-like snowdrops, standing in little groups together. And not far off you will perhaps see something that looks just like a shrivelled brown leaf. It *may* be a dead leaf, of course, but if it scuttles away fast when you bend down, you'll know what it really is – old Dame Bonnet herself!

Tammylin's friend

Once upon a time there was a little pixie who didn't like earwigs. Now this was very silly because earwigs are clean and tidy creatures and never mind doing a good turn for the fairies.

Still, Tammylin the pixie couldn't bear an earwig near her, and whenever she saw one she always sent it scurrying away in fright. She kept a little broom which she used specially for frightening earwigs, and she often used to sweep away any that came near her neat little house and garden.

Now one day when Tammylin was wandering in the violet wood all by herself, humming a song and dancing round the sweet-smelling violets, she

walked quite by mistake into the Green
Magician's garden.

He lived in the middle of the wood,
and as he had no wall or fence or hedge
round his garden, it was very difficult
to see it. Tammylin didn't see it at all
– and she walked right into it just as
the Green Magician was coming out to
do his shopping!

"Oho!" he said, and caught hold
of Tammylin, who was alarmed and

astonished. "So you've come spying round, have you, to see what kind of secret magic I make? Well, you'll be sorry now! You can be my cook. The rabbit who waited on me has just left to get married – you will do nicely instead."

"I won't, I won't!" squealed Tammylin, and she wriggled as hard as she could. But it wasn't a bit of good. The Green Magician wrapped her up in his green cloak and took her into his cottage. He cut off her pretty silver wings and gave her an apron to wear.

"My wings won't grow for three weeks," sobbed Tammylin. "You are very horrid. I shall run away as soon as you've gone out."

"Oh, no, you won't!" said the Green Magician – and what do you think he did? He took his magic wand, waved it round his garden seven times and called out a magic word – and lo and behold! a great wall grew round it, so high that Tammylin couldn't see the top.

"There," said the magician, pleased. "What do you think of that? You can't escape now."

He went out to do his shopping, unlocking and locking a big door in the wall. Tammylin was left alone to cook the dinner. How she wished she could let her friends know where she was!

When the Green Magician went to market, he heard everyone talking about Tammylin's disappearance, but he didn't say a word. No, he had got a cook for nothing, and he meant to keep her. He went to the fish-stall and bought some herrings. He went to the sweet-stall and bought some peppermints. He went to the fruit-stall and there he bought some pears and a large cauliflower.

He carried them all home in his big bag, and went in through the door in the wall again, locking it after him. He put his shopping down on the kitchen table and told Tammylin to cook the cauliflower for dinner.

"I'm going into the garden to water my flowers," he said. So out he went, and left Tammylin to get on with the cooking. The little pixie sulkily took up the cauliflower – and as she did so, out crept a very large earwig. Tammylin dropped the cauliflower with a shriek.

"Hello, Tammylin," said the earwig in surprise. "How did you come to be here?"

"The Green Magician caught me," said Tammylin, "and I can't escape because there's a high wall round the garden and my wings are cut off. Oh, go away, you horrid earwig! If only you were a butterfly you could fly up over the wall and tell everyone where I am. Then my friends would rescue me. What a pity you are such an ugly, useless earwig."

"You are unkind, Tammylin," said the earwig.

Just then the Green Magician poked his head in at the window. "Who are you talking to?" he said.

"To an earwig, the horrid thing!" said Tammylin.

"Oh, an earwig," said the Magician. "Well, *he's* a prisoner here too – he can crawl around the garden but he can't get out. If it had been a butterfly, a bee, or a moth I'd have stopped him from taking any message to your friends. But an earwig has no wings."

As soon as the magician had gone back to the garden the earwig ran close to Tammylin and began to whisper.

"Listen, Tammylin, the magician is wrong," it said. "I *have* got wings."

Tammylin stared in surprise at the brown, smooth-backed earwig. "You haven't!" she said. "What a storyteller you are!"

"Sh!" said the earwig. "I tell you I *have* got wings. I keep them neatly folded under my back-shell. Look, those brown things on my back are my wing-cases. Watch how I unfold my beautiful gauzy wings."

Tammylin watched in the greatest

astonishment. The earwig lifted up his
brown wing-cases from his back and
shook out his wings. They were gauzy
like a bee's, but long and beautifully
folded – just like a fan.

The earwig spread them out. "I'm
going off to tell your friends where

you are," he said. "They will rescue you soon. Goodbye."

Tammylin watched the earwig fly up into the air on his long gauzy wings, up, up and up – right over the wall. The Green Magician never even saw him.

"Well," thought Tammylin, washing the cauliflower, "I never knew before that earwigs had wings folded so beautifully under their back-shells. How kind of him to fly off to tell my friends. I wish I hadn't been so horrid to earwigs. I never will be again!"

The earwig flew straight to the market-place, folded his wings neatly, poked them tidily under his back-shell with his pincers, and then told everyone where he had seen Tammylin. It wasn't long before the King himself, at the head of twenty men, was riding through the violet wood to rescue Tammylin. But as soon as the Magician heard his King's voice he took down the wall, and fled away to the borders of Fairyland. He knew that it was forbidden to capture pixies.

"But how, how, *how* did the King know where Tammylin was?" he wondered a hundred times a day. He never knew – but Tammylin did not forget her kind friend.

"I will never chase earwigs away again," she said. "I didn't know they were so kind, and had such lovely wings, folded like fans."

"Oh, earwigs are good people," said the King, as she rode back safely with him. "They look after their little ones as few insects do – they are very good mothers. You should not be unkind to anything, Tammylin. Goodness and loveliness may be found in even the ugliest creatures. You never know!"

Now Tammylin is friends with all the earwigs, beetles and spiders that she knows, and never dreams of using her broom to sweep them away. Wasn't it a good thing for her that an earwig had wings! Did *you* know that?

She couldn't remember

"Winnie, you've left the door open again!" called Mummy.

"Bother!" said Winnie, and came back to shut it. "I wish I could remember. I'm always forgetting."

"You should try a little harder to remember," said Mummy. "Goodbye, dear. Hurry, or you'll be late for school."

Winnie banged the front door and ran to the gate. She opened it – and forgot to shut it. Mother knocked on the window.

"Winnie! Winnie! Shut the gate! The dogs will come in and spoil the garden."

But Winnie didn't hear. She was half-way down the road. She really was dreadful about forgetting to shut doors and gates. She just couldn't remember!

She ran to school. She was rather late, so she quickly changed her shoes in the cloakroom and then slipped into her classroom to take her place.

Of course she left the door open! "Do shut the door, Winnie!" said Miss Brown. "One of these days you'll forget to shut a door or a gate, and you'll be very sorry indeed!"

Of course Winnie didn't believe that! It was the sort of thing that grown-ups always said. But wait a minute, Winnie. This time Miss Brown is right – you'll be very sorry indeed next time you leave a door or a gate open!

On the next Saturday Winnie was very pleased because her Auntie Alice had asked her to go to tea. She loved going to Auntie Alice's cottage. It was in the country, and there were plenty of flowers and fruit trees in the garden. Sometimes it was strawberry-time, sometimes there were raspberries to pick, and there were plums, apples and pears later in the year.

"It's apple and pear time now," thought Winnie, as she got ready to go. "Auntie will let me pick plenty, I know, and she'll tell me to take a bagful home. What fun!"

"Winnie, put on your new blue hat!" called Mummy. "Auntie will like to see that. And take your blue scarf too, and your blue handkerchief. Then you will look very nice."

"Ooh, yes!" said Winnie, delighted. So she put on her new blue straw hat with the white daisies round it, and put her blue scarf round her neck. She stuffed her blue handkerchief into her pocket, leaving one end out to show a little. She really did look nice!

Off she went. Auntie Alice was delighted to see her. "You can go to that red apple tree and pick two nice ripe apples to eat," she said to Winnie.

As Winnie was going to the red apple tree, she noticed that all the Michaelmas Daisy plants nearby were cut down before they had even flowered.

"Oh, Auntie, why have you cut them down?" she asked, in disappointment. "I was so looking forward to seeing them all in flower!"

"Well, darling, you left the gate open last time you went home, after seeing me," said Auntie sadly. "And two cows got into the garden and trampled down all my lovely daisies. So we had to cut down the poor broken stalks."

"Oh, Auntie, I'm so sorry," said Winnie, ashamed of herself.

"I think that until something punishes you hard for leaving gates open, you will never remember," said Auntie. "Just see if you can be a good, thoughtful girl today and shut every gate you go through! It is very important in the country."

Well, Winnie remembered to shut the orchard gate. She remembered to shut the field gate when she went through it to look for blackberries. She remembered to shut them both when she came back too. She felt quite

pleased with herself.

But do you know what she didn't do, when she went in to tea? She quite forgot to shut the garden gate that led into the lane! Outside in the lane were two old goats belonging to Mrs Brown up the road. They were always on the look-out for open gates, because they loved eating the flowers and vegetables in a garden – they tasted much nicer than grass in the lane!

When Auntie called Winnie in to tea, the little girl was pleased, for she was very hungry. She had been sitting reading a new story book that Auntie had given her. On the grass beside her were two more books, her new hat, her blue scarf, her handkerchief, and a big bagful of ripe apples.

She jumped up, leaving everything neatly together, and ran into the house. And whilst Winnie was having *her* tea, those two goats came in at the open gate and had *their* tea!

And what do you think they ate for their tea? They ate one new hat, one blue scarf, one blue handkerchief, three story books, twenty-two ripe apples, *and* the bag they were in!

Goats will eat anything – but this was a wonderful tea for them. How they enjoyed it! Nobody knew anything about it till Winnie looked out of the window and saw one of the goats walking about on the lawn, with a bit of her blue scarf hanging out of its mouth. It was just finishing a good chew.

"Oh!" screamed poor Winnie. "Look! That goat is eating my scarf! Quick, Auntie, stop him!"

They rushed out – but it was too late to stop the goats. Everything was inside them! Auntie Alice shooed them angrily away, and then turned to comfort poor Winnie, who was sobbing bitterly.

"They've eaten my new hat with the daisies," sobbed Winnie, "and my scarf and hanky, and my new books, and all my apples! And I haven't time to pick any more because it is time for the bus. Mother will be so cross about my hat! Oh, those horrid, horrid goats! How did they get in?"

"Winnie," said Auntie, in a grave sort of voice, "they got in through the open gate – but who left the gate open?"

Winnie sobbed even more loudly. "I did!" she wept. "It's my own fault. But oh, don't scold me any more because I am so unhappy!"

So Auntie said no more, but took poor Winnie to the bus and put her in, still crying. Mummy wondered whatever the matter was when she saw her little girl coming home with red eyes and tear-stained cheeks.

Winnie soon told her everything. Mummy wasn't cross. She just said, "Well, Winnie, I knew this sort of thing would happen sooner or later. I can't afford to buy you a new hat or scarf. You must wear your old ones again. It's a good thing I haven't given them away."

So Winnie is wearing her old hat and scarf again now, and she feels very sad when she sees all the other children wearing their new ones. When she sees them she frowns and says to herself, "I will always remember to shut doors and gates behind me." And I rather think she will now, don't you?

The lost princess

Once upon a time there was a poor page-boy called Gladsome. He was the youngest of seven sons, and had been brought up to be a well-mannered page. But the prince he served was killed in a fight, so the little page-boy was left to seek for his fortune alone.

He tied up his few belongings in a bundle, put them on the end of his stout stick, and set off. For many months he wandered here and there, but nowhere could he find a master who wanted a page. Soon he came to another land, and after much travelling arrived at the chief city.

In the midst of this city was a towering palace. Its spires rose into the clouds, and when the sun shone brightly, it looked like gold. The King of that country lived there with his wife, the beautiful Queen. Gladsome took heart when he saw the palace, for he thought that here, surely, there would be many nobles who would like to have a well-mannered page-boy.

He went to the palace, and was admitted. He asked all the lords he saw if he could be page to them, but one and all shook their heads. Not a smile did Gladsome get, and he walked out of the palace again, feeling very miserable.

"What is the matter with everyone here?" he asked the gate-keeper. "They look as gloomy as owls."

"Hush!" said the gate-keeper. "You must be a stranger. Do you not know our sorrow?"

"No," said Gladsome, in wonder. "What is it?"

"We have lost our Princess!" whispered the gate-keeper. "Isn't it dreadful? She was playing in the woods one day and was spirited away, no one knows where. We haven't heard a word of her since."

"What a strange thing!" said Gladsome, and he walked out, thinking deeply. When he got outside, he saw a big notice on the wall. He went up and read it. This is what it said:

Lost – a beautiful princess. Anyone finding her will be rewarded with a thousand bags of gold and half the kingdom.

"Now just think of that!" said the youth to himself. "There's a fortune for you!"

He spoke to the people of the town and they told him that many princes had come from all over the world to try and win the reward. They had gone to wizards and enchanters, goblins and magicians, but nowhere had they found the Princess. Many of them had lost their lives, or had been forced to become slaves to the goblins, and now no one ever came to try their luck, for it was said that never would the lovely Princess be found.

"Well, I'll try *my* luck!" said the page-boy. "I can't find work to do, so I might as well take this job on instead."

"Foolish youth!" said the towns-people. "Are you vain enough to think that you are more clever than princes?"

"Perhaps I am, and perhaps I'm not!" said Gladsome. "But tell me, good folk, what part of this land is very little

known, for methinks that there, maybe, the Princess is hidden?"

"Go to the west as far as the mountains," said an old man. "There is a narrow pass over them, known to none nowadays. Maybe you can find it. On the other side of the mountains is a thick forest in which many a prince has lost his life. In it lives a dwarf who is said to know everything."

"Then I will go and ask him if he will tell me where the Princess is!" cried the youth.

And boldly he shouldered his bundle, and set off, whilst the towns-folk looked after him, and shook their heads.

For ten days and ten nights the youth kept to the west, and at last he came to the high mountains. He climbed up them, panting for breath, but nowhere could he see a way to pass over them.

At last, feeling very thirsty, he looked about for a spring. He saw one, gushing out from above a high rock. It was difficult to get to, but he managed it at last. He drank from it, and found it very good. Then he climbed down again, and looked about for a cave in which he might pass the night.

As he searched, he heard a voice speaking to him, and he turned in surprise. Nearby was an old woman, carrying a jug.

"Kind sir," she said, "my spring has dried up, and I cannot reach the one from which I saw you drink just now. Will you fill my jug for me?"

Now Gladsome was tired, and it was hard work climbing up the rock to the spring. But he said nothing of this, and took the old woman's jug from her with a smile. He climbed up to fill it with water, and soon returned to her. She thanked him kindly, and then, to his great astonishment, emptied the clear water all over herself!

In a trice she had changed to a beautiful fairy, and she laughed to see the youth's amazement.

"I asked you for water just to try

you," she said. "I know the way over the mountains, but I tell my secret only to those who are kind of heart. No one has given me so sweet a smile as you!"

"This is a strange thing!" said Gladsome, hardly able to believe his eyes. He had heard of fairies and goblins, enchanters and wizards often enough, but this was the first time he had seen one of them with his own eyes.

"Come to my cave," said the fairy. "You shall spend the night there, and I will give you a good meal, for you look hungry."

Gladsome went with her, and she showed him a magnificent cave, hung with wonderful curtains and carpeted with velvet. Little elves waited on them, and soon the youth was enjoying a delicious feast.

"I seek the lost Princess," said Gladsome. "Do you know where she is?"

"No," said the fairy. "Many princes have asked me that. All of them went over the pass, but none came back. I warn you to go back, Gladsome, while there is yet time."

"I must go on," said the youth. "Tell me of this dwarf who lives in the forest."

"He is a dreadful creature," said the fairy, with a shudder. "He will take you prisoner I have no doubt, and then you will be his slave for ever."

"Oh no, I shan't," said the youth. "I hope I'm a match for any dwarf. How can I find my way through the forest?"

"There is a silver cord running right through it," answered the fairy. "If you hold on to that, you will come to the other end safely. But if you let go for one moment to follow anyone into the forest, you will never find the cord again."

"That seems easy enough to do," said Gladsome, and he made up his mind to start out again the very next morning. He slept soundly in a bed of flower-petals, and when the sun rose the fairy woke him.

"I will show you the way over the

mountains," she said. "Come with me."

He followed her to where a great rock stood. The fairy pushed it a little, and it swung to one side. Behind it lay a passage right through the mountain.

"I should never have found this by myself," thought Gladsome. He and the fairy went through, and soon came out on the other side of the mountain. Below lay a thick, dark forest.

"Listen," said the fairy. "I dare not walk with you any further, but I will do something else for you. I will fly over the forest to the other side, and wait for you there. I will wait until sunrise tomorrow, so do not be late. And whatever you do, *don't* leave the silver cord or you will be lost for ever."

"Goodbye," said Gladsome, gratefully. "I'll be sure to meet you tomorrow at sunrise."

He ran down the path, and after some time he came to the forest. Tied to a tree by the path was a thick silver cord that gleamed in the darkness of the forest like a live thing. Gladsome took hold of it and went along the path through the gloomy trees.

After he had walked for some time, and the forest had become darker and darker, Gladsome saw a little man standing behind a tree.

"Who are you?" he called. "Are you the dwarf that lives in this forest?"

"I am," answered the dwarf, in a hoarse voice. "Do you want to know where the Princess is?"

"Yes," said Gladsome. "Can you tell me?"

"Come and have a glass of nectar with me, and I'll tell you everything," answered the dwarf.

"Aha!" thought Gladsome. "He wants me to leave the silver cord, for he knows I shan't be able to find my way back. Well, I'll defeat his little plan!"

Swiftly he took a ball of string from his pocket, and tied the end of it to the silver cord. He put the string back into his pocket again, and kept his hand on top of it, so that he could unwind the string without being seen. The dwarf was too far away to see what he was doing, but he kept calling to Gladsome all the time.

"Come along, come along! I'll tell you all you want to know, young man. I can give you nectar to drink that cannot be bettered by the King of Fairyland!"

"I'm coming," said Gladsome, and he stepped away from the silver cord, and went up to where the dwarf stood.

"Walk in front of me and show me the way. The path is too narrow for two abreast."

The dwarf turned and ran chuckling through the trees. As he went, Gladsome unwound his string, and felt very glad to think that the other end was safely tied to the silver cord. By following his own string back again, he could find the silver cord whenever he wished!

At last they came to a dark little cave, and here the dwarf sat down with Gladsome. He gave him a glass of yellow nectar to drink, but the youth quietly poured it into the ground when the dwarf had turned away his head; for he guessed that there was something in the drink that would make him fall asleep, and so put himself in the little man's power.

"Now tell me where the lost Princess is," said Gladsome.

The dwarf threw back his head and laughed loudly.

"Foolish boy," he said, grinning wickedly. "You are easy to deceive. You have left the silver cord and will never be able to find your way back again. So I gain another servant! The nectar I gave you will make you heavy with sleep in a few moments, and then I shall bind you, and bid my slaves carry you away!"

Gladsome pretended to be very frightened and he begged the dwarf for mercy. The little man laughed all the more.

"Well, I don't believe you know where

the lost Princess is, for all you say that you do," said Gladsome, pretending to yawn.

"Oho, don't I!" said the dwarf. "Well, I'll just tell you everything, before you go off into a magic sleep! Then perhaps you'll believe me. Listen. The Princess was carried away by the enchanter who lives in the castle at the other end of this forest. That is why he put me here to prevent all the princes from going there. But no one can get into the castle unseen unless he wears the magical golden scarf on his shoulders. That scarf will make him invisible."

"Nonsense," said Gladsome, pretending to be half asleep. "I don't believe in such a thing!"

The dwarf fell into a fury. He rushed to the back of his cave, and came back with a beautiful scarf of purest gold. He threw it over his shoulders and – hey presto! – he had disappeared. He took it off, and there he was again.

"Do you believe me now?" he asked angrily.

"Yes, yes," said Gladsome, pretending to fall back asleep. He watched the dwarf hang the scarf on a nail, and then the little man came and looked at him closely. Gladsome pretended to snore.

"Aha, another one!" said the dwarf, rubbing his hands together. "I'll take a nap myself, I think."

He lay down, and soon snores came from his open mouth.

Gladsome sat up. Then, quietly, he rose to his feet and ran to get the scarf off the peg. He threw it over his shoulders and crept by the sleeping dwarf. He ran his fingers along the string that he had unwound when he had followed the dwarf and began winding it up again. As he wound it he followed it, and soon he came to the silver cord. Then once more he set out through the forest.

He travelled for many hours all

through the night, always following the cord. No one met him and the youth felt lonely. But as the time drew near for the sun to rise once more his heart felt lighter. The forest was getting thinner, and soon he saw the end of it! As he reached the last tree the sun rose in the eastern sky, and to his joy the fairy was waiting for him.

"You have done well," she said, when she had heard his adventures. "Now come with me and we will go to the castle which the dwarf told you about. It must be that one, over to the west."

They soon arrived there, and the youth put the golden scarf over his shoulders to make himself invisible.

"I will stay somewhere near by, in case you need help," whispered the fairy.

Unseen by the gate-keeper, the youth slipped in through the gates and found himself in a beautiful garden. He quickly ran through it until he came to the door of the castle itself. It was open

and twelve footmen stood by it. They did not see the youth run by, for he still had the magic scarf on his shoulders and was invisible.

Gladsome looked into this room and that room, and then ran upstairs. Seated at the window of a tower room was the lost Princess! She looked very sad. The enchanter sat at a table near by, studying a strange book.

Gladsome ran lightly up to the

Princess and whispered in her ear. "Do not be afraid. I am Gladsome, a youth come to save you. I am wearing a magic scarf which makes me invisible. Go to the garden as soon as you can, and I will meet you there."

The Princess turned pale when she heard those words whispered from the empty air. Then she turned red with joy. The enchanter had heard nothing. She rose, and went up to him.

"I am going to walk in the garden," she said.

"Go then," said the enchanter. "But remember that I will marry you tonight, whether you wish it or not. I have waited long enough."

The maiden ran down the stairs, and went out into the garden. Gladsome lightly followed her, and when they were safely behind a thick bush, he took off the magic scarf and showed himself.

"I will put it round both of us," he said, joyfully. "Then we can slip out of the gate unseen!"

But alas for him! At that very moment the wind blew strongly, and the magic scarf flew into the air. Gladsome raced after it, but try as he might, he could not catch it. At last it became caught on the topmost branch of a high tree, and the youth saw that he would have to climb up and get it.

Now at that moment the enchanter happened to look out of the window. What he saw amazed him very much. He drew back the curtain, and saw the Princess crying in fear, and Gladsome just about to climb a tree.

"Now what is this?" cried the enchanter, and he drew his sword and rushed down the stairs.

Poor Gladsome was captured, and the Princess trembled when she thought he might be slain. The enchanter was furious, and he made the youth enter the castle at the point of his sword.

"So!" he said. "You would come to rescue the Princess, my bold youth! Then I will marry her this minute, and as a wedding gift I will give her your head afterwards!"

He rang a bell, and bade his servants make ready for the marriage. When all was prepared he dragged the Princess forward, and was just about to put a ring on her finger, when a strange thing happened. She disappeared!

The enchanter looked here and there, but he could see her nowhere! He looked to see if Gladsome had done anything to make her vanish, and when he saw the youth looking most astonished he rushed at him to slay him.

But Gladstone disappeared too! The enchanter bellowed and shouted, and his servants raced up and down and to and fro – but all to no purpose. The Princess and the bold youth had both completely gone!

Where were they? Ah, they were quite safe! The fairy had seen to that. She had seen the magic scarf blow off Gladsome's shoulders, and had watched him being captured. Then, when the garden was empty, she had flown to the tree where the scarf still rested, and had taken it. She flew into the castle, and dropped it around the Princess's shoulders just in time. And, of course, when the Princess found herself invisible, she at once ran to Gladsome, and put half of the scarf round *his* shoulders too!

It was easy to escape from the castle then. They ran out together, and slipped out of the gate. Then, with the fairy to show them the right way, they hastened back to the dark forest. In safety they followed the silver cord, for the dwarf could not see them now, and at last they came to the passage through the mountains.

"Goodbye," said Gladsome to the fairy. "I do hope you'll come and visit us some day."

"Come to our wedding!" said the Princess; for she had already made up her mind that Gladsome was the husband for her. Never had she seen anyone so brave!

What rejoicing there was when the two arrived safely at the King's palace! How the bells rang! How the people shouted! What wedding preparations there were!